Tina,

Thin

Veils

Anne Hanson

Stay healthy...
Be happy
Anne Hanson
2/15/2021

This book is a work of fiction. Places, events, and situations in this story are purely fictional. Any resemblance to actual persons, living or dead, is coincidental.

© 2003 by Anne Hanson. All rights reserved.

No part of this book may be reproduced, stored in a retrieval system, or transmitted by any means, electronic, mechanical, photocopying, recording, or otherwise, without written permission from the author.

ISBN: 1-4107-2746-7 (e-book)
ISBN: 1-4107-2747-5 (Paperback)

Library of Congress Control Number: 2003091496

This book is printed on acid free paper.

Printed in the United States of America
Bloomington, IN

First published in 1999 by Windsor House Publishing Group, Inc.

1stBooks - rev. 5/02/03

Dedication

To my mother and to my father,
who always called me *his* writer.

Acknowledgments

I wish to thank the following people whose inspiration and guidance helped produce my book: my sisters, family, and friends; my niece, Laurie Prichard, authors, Penny Porter and Pam Spencer; eating disorder specialist, Eleanor Gross; librarians Meredeth Mcgowan and Cynthia Robinson; husband and friend, George Hanson.

Prologue

Before I wake, I pray the Lord my soul to take. Erica lay facing the ceiling, embracing her arms. She stroked the sleeves of her satiny nightgown while thinking her prayers. God bless Mom and Philip and Grandpa Flanagan. Take care of Daddy, Grandma and Kim. And Kim. Erica paused. Had she actually been expecting Kim's death that her name found its way onto her prayer list so easily?

Erica had searched anxiously for the nightgown she now wore, finding the almost-forgotten present crumpled in the corner of her seldom opened bottom dresser drawer. Normally she wore a tee-shirt to bed, but tomorrow was Kim's funeral and Erica needed to clothe herself in something soft and formal though she didn't know why.

The flannel lining caressed her body as she drew each breath in. And out. Its delicate touch would have comforted her had she been willing to accept comfort. I tried to help you Kim, I swear. You wouldn't let me, why wouldn't you let me? Erica hurried to her feet, her breaths now unsteady heaves. She grabbed at the carefully set comforter and sheet and thrust her body beneath them. The shivering, so sudden, frightened her. She drew her knees toward her chest, clasped them tightly and rocked.

Oh Kim, Kimmy, I miss you. The tightness of the nightgown's sleeves pinching Erica's armpits forced her to release her knees. Nightgown's a little snug, huh, Kimmy? Think I need to lose a little weight?

Tears Erica could barely believe remained wet the pillow she now used to smother her sobs. "Oh, Kimmy, you're dead. You're dead."

Erica turned and wiped her eyes roughly with her fist. She found her original position, righting her nightgown and tugging at the wrinkled sleeves until they fit her arms once again. She stared at the ceiling, then at the dress draped over her rocking chair. The sensible dress she had planned to wear to the dance. Now she would wear it to Kim's funeral. Her eyes moved to the picture hanging above the chair. She recalled the time when she had studied that picture, hoping to interpret its clues to the puzzle she solved too late. The time when she first suspected Kim was in trouble. It really wasn't that long ago.

I
The Note

"If I see you look at that note one more time, Kim, I'm taking it," Mrs. Carlson yelled. It wasn't really a yell. Erica knew that. It was more like a threat. But Erica felt too sorry for her best friend Kim to care about the difference.

Kim had unfolded that stupid note three separate times! The first time Erica barely noticed, but Mrs. Carlson had. Strolling over to Kim, Mrs. Carlson had leaned forward and whispered something that made Kim fold the note and slip it into her shirt pocket. The second time, Erica realized her teacher was trying to help Kim stay out of trouble. Reading aloud from Ray Bradbury's *Dandelion Wine,* Mrs. Carlson praised its descriptive language while simultaneously supervising the note's return to the pocket from which Kim had plucked it with tweezer-like fingers. "Nice try, Kim," was what Erica, seated next to Kim, barely heard her teacher say.

After the third confrontation, the *threat*, when Erica thought for certain her teacher would issue Kim a detention, Mrs. Carlson instead arched an eyebrow and flashed an almost imperceptible glare at Kim. "Now where was I?" she needlessly asked then answered dramatically, "Ah yes. Here's another wonderful passage I'd like to read to you."

Erica's mouth watered as she listened to a description of intoxicating aromas that filled the kitchen of a young boy's grandmother. Suddenly Mrs. Carlson shouted: "Kim!"

Kim had gone too far. Why did she open that stupid note again? Mrs. Carlson was trying to be fair. Weeks ago, Erica had spent her first days as a high school student sizing up each of her teachers. She knew that Carlson was okay once you got past her it's-the-beginning-of-school-so-I-have-to-be-mean act. She also knew that Mrs. Carlson did not make idle threats. Erica felt nervous, confused and angry all at once. Kim wouldn't have risked getting into trouble unless that note was important—really important. And now Kim lost the note completely because Mrs. Carlson stormed down the aisle, grabbed it, and declared: "Now maybe this nonsense will end."

Slouching in her chair, Erica chomped on her pen top nervously. Who wrote that note? she wondered. And what does it say that's so important? Kim has been acting weird lately. Even for Kim. Quiet. Distant. Snobby, almost. Erica sighed, troubled that no matter how hard she had tried to get her best friend—or at least she thought her best friend—to tell her what was the matter, Kim had refused. The last time Erica asked what was wrong, Kim had snapped, "Nothing is wrong…now leave me alone. Please!"

Erica knew to leave Kim alone (although now she wished she hadn't). Kim was her "moody" friend. After Kim had gone home from the first of countless sleepovers, Erica's mother had commented that Kim seemed like the pensive type. Erica searched for the word in her dictionary and upon finding it knew the word fit Kim perfectly. She even felt a little smug knowing someone who was pensive. But that was not the best word to describe her. No.

Kim's family had rented a house in Erica's neighborhood during fifth grade. Erica had immediately suspected that her new neighbor, Kim Spencer, held some dark secret—adoption, kidnapping—something exciting. She had called on Jeanna, her *first* best friend. "That new girl Kim is strange. She never rides the bus with us. What's with her?"

"She must be shy, that's all. She hasn't even made a single friend at school."

"Well, I think we should try to help her feel welcome."

By the time that school year had ended and the Spencers had moved into their luxurious home in Glenhill Estates, Erica knew Kim lamented the loss of her bus ride time home with her two new and best friends.

Now, four years later, Erica knew Kim was not shy. And she found it downright irritating that Kim—her soon to be "former" best friend if she didn't change her more than usual snooty attitude—was not acting pensive or shy: she was rude!

Erica's restless fingers rotated her pen between her teeth as disturbing questions invaded her thoughts. Could that letter mean that maybe Kim's in some kind of trouble?…Could it…it couldn't be *that* kind of trouble. Erica gasped and her pen dropped to the floor.

"Erica, are you okay? Do you need to get some water?"

"Wha, huh?...Oh, no, Mrs. Carlson. I just coughed a little." A blush tingled her face as she cleared her throat and shifted her body upright in her seat. What's going on? Oh gawd...I don't even know what I'm supposed to be doing! Frantically she eyed nearby notebooks. She saw circles with words written inside. Immediately she drew a large circle on the clean page in her notebook which, till that moment, merely contained: 9/14: Using Adjectives To. She had stopped there. To do what, she wondered. Write descriptively? Creatively? She concluded that the circle must at least need some adjectives. Erica quickly scribbled *delicious*, *sparkling*, then *stupid* into her circle. She searched her mind for more adjectives, found the word *curious*, and as she wrote it, decided that Kim would have a lot of explaining to do as soon as eighth period was over. Erica would demand to know what was in that note!

"Before you leave today," Mrs. Carlson almost shouted over the pre-dismissal noise, "I have been asked to remind dance committee members that you are meeting with the student council tomorrow to discuss the Freshman Harvest Dance. Is there anyone here on that committee?" Several students raised their hands while others responded by calling out to Mrs. Carlson.

"I am."

"Right here."

"Yo."

Determined to squeeze her notebook into her overstuffed bag Erica continued the pursuit with her right hand while raising her left. "Me," she added meekly.

THIN VEILS

Pleased that so many of her new freshmen were involved, Mrs. Carlson smiled. "Good. Good," she said. "Please gather your ideas tonight..." Dropping her tone and raising her eyebrow she added, "*after* you do all your homework. And if you haven't any ideas," she teased, "I suggest you stimulate the creative energies within your minds, because the council *is* expecting ideas."

The bell rang and Erica rushed through the crowded hall to find Kim. Normally Kim, Erica, and Jeanna waited for each other. Not today. Today, Kim disappeared in the swarm of bodies that surged toward the nearest exit. Erica didn't even think of Jeanna as she hurried after Kim, finally catching her by her locker. "Hey," she shouted. "Are you crazy or something? Why didn't you wait for me and Jeanna? What's with that note? I thought Carlson was gonna give you a detention for taking it out so many times. Who sent it to you? Are you nuts or—"

"Leave me alone, all right?" Kim hollered, jolting Erica into wide-eyed, open-mouthed silence. "Just shut up and leave me alone!"

Ignoring the bodies that roughly shoved past her, Erica watched Kim storm away. Yes, Erica knew she talked too much; she was everyone's "motor-mouth" friend. But never had Kim, nor any of her other friends for that matter, spoken to her so sharply. Something was wrong. Very wrong. And it had to do with that note.

✸✸✸✸✸✸✸

The bus ride home seemed endless. Erica's indifference at missing the early bus stayed with her as she stared vacantly out the clean window. She would have been glad the adjacent seats remained empty had she been able to feel anything. But she could not. Silence. Silence filled her. Not anger. Anger never even crossed her mind. *Something's wrong with my best friend, and I don't know what it is.*

Erica reviewed the days and weeks prior to today, searching for clues. She caught glimpses of isolated incidents that had meant so little at the time they had occurred. *Kim just being her moody-snooty self.*

The first glimpse occurred as the bus rode past Glenhill Park. She remembered herself sitting on the ball field with several of her best friends. They had been excitedly discussing their upcoming year as high school freshman when Steve suggested they go somewhere to eat. "Good idea. What do we feel like?" Erica did not remember who had replied first, only that when she suggested the donut shop, Kim screeched, "Gawd, Erica. You look like that and you want to eat donuts?"

Erica closed her eyes, trying to blur the details of the too sharp memory. But the echo of Kim's laughing response to Erica's shocked silence found her and now haunted her: "Oh, Erica, lighten up...I was just kidding." Her face burned red. *How do you insult your best friend like that* she wondered *and then just slough it off as kidding?* Reminded of her lame retort, "At least I'm not a beanpole like you, Kim," Erica winced. Ugh. Aside from shaking her confidence, the memory served no apparent purpose but to direct Erica to a more recent confrontation.

There she sat on Kim's front porch finding it impossible to ignore the shouting she heard from inside the house. The door slammed. "Kim!" Erica had turned and protested. "You're not going to leave, are you? How can you yell at your mother like that and then just storm out of the house?"

"Get up, Erica," she snapped, punctuating each word that followed, "because we are leaving." Erica would have preferred to forget the rest. "And as for yelling at my mother, what can I tell you, Erica? I'm not perfect like you…you…your mother…your brother…you're all perfect. Maybe you should give lessons on how to be the perfect family."

Erica rubbed her forehead and frowned. Why had she let Kim talk to her that way? The divorce was old news. And the patience she had extended to Kim during her parents turbulent separation process was as ignored as it was abundant. Why did she always allow her feelings to take a back seat to Kim's? Disheartened, she collapsed her head softly onto the window. She regretted how vividly she had recalled the incidents filled with sarcasm and cruelty, but followed by apologies so sincere, Erica felt guilty she recalled the apologies only vaguely.

The bus stopped. If there were more to recall, there was no time. Erica grabbed the back of the seat in front of her, hoisted her body upward and walked slowly to the exit door.

II
Secret Diet

The keys jingled teasingly as Erica assaulted her bag to find them. She had to get those keys. Get inside her house. Call Jeanna—all her friends if necessary—until she found the one who might help her figure out what was going on with Kim. Suddenly the door flung wide open, the knob whacking into the wall behind it. "I got three stars today! Three green stars!"

Philip's excitement couldn't have been more unwelcome yet Erica smiled. "Oh wow, Philip, that's great." Erica's five-year-old brother jumped up as she bent down to lift his sturdy body. He planted an oatmeal cookie kiss on her flushed cheek and she heaved a sigh. She lowered him to stand and kissed the crown of his silky brown hair. As she straightened up, she reluctantly shifted her priorities. "That's really great, Philip. I'm proud of you...Your bus got you home early today. Are you wearing your key?"

Philip frowned then bit his tongue as he groped under his striped sweatshirt for the end of his leather cord necklace. "Here it is," he grumbled. "You know that."

Philip's pout tugged at Erica and she knelt down before him. "I'm sorry, baby. You know I have to check. And, well...hey, I think it's pretty terrific that you got...how many?...three stars in one day!" His smile returned. Closing her eyes, Erica hugged Philip warmly. As she stroked his back, an unexpected memory from last spring rang in her ears: "Your brother is so obnoxious."

Kim had visited Erica to do homework but left abruptly complaining, "I'm the one who came all the way over here and you're paying more attention to him than me. You're as obnoxious as he is the way you baby him!" The accusation had disturbed Erica deeply, so similar it was to the one with which she sometimes indicted herself. But she didn't know any other way to be a big sister.

Weaving this memory together with the others produced a disturbing pattern and an embrace which lingered too long. When Erica finally released Philip and rested back on her heels, she saw beyond his smile to the uneasy look in his eyes. She forced a grin and then a silly face which Philip immediately mimicked. Good. That's over with. Erica stood up, turned, and in a leap bounded up the first two steps of the staircase. Soon she'd be in her room, on her phone, tracking down answers.

"Don't ya wanna see my stars, Erica?"

Erica halted, frozen or melted (she was never quite sure which) by her baby brother. Her head slumped back on her shoulders. She stared at her room at the top of the stairs and muttered a whimpering cry, softly enough so Philip couldn't hear. Her room—and her mission—would have to wait.

"Sure I want to see your stars, Philip." She turned and stomped heavily down the stairs, the weight of each step punctuating her words. "I just didn't know you wanted to show me before Mom got home." She could almost hear Kim's snicker as she lied.

Reaching for Erica's hand, Philip guided her down the last plush blue-carpeted step, through the hallway, and into the kitchen. He rushed over to his green nylon backpack which lay in sharp contrast on the white kitchen counter. Philip's tongue inched across his lips slowly and deliberately as he opened the zipper. "I got it right here...Here it is! Here! See!"

He held up a piece of almost neatly folded red construction paper. Ceremoniously Erica unfolded his collage of the four food groups and fussed, "Oho, look at that. Three stars. Philip, that's great! I'm going to put it right here on the front of the refrigerator so Mom can see it when she gets home. She's going to be so excited." Erica quickly opened the clamp on one of many refrigerator magnets—this one a brown gingerbread man—and shoved the top of Philip's project between plastic feet that clicked shut.

"There!" she pronounced, marching out of the kitchen after brushing another kiss atop Philip's head. Nine years his senior, Erica was aware that sometimes she felt as though Philip were her son instead of her brother. And in spite of what anyone said—especially Kim!—Erica assured herself she liked the feeling.

Finally in her room, Erica flung her books on her bed and collapsed beside them. She lunged for her phone and dialed Jeanna. "Jeanna? Hi, it's me...What's with Kim?...I'm sorry I didn't wait for you...Well, I just couldn't wait! I had to go after Kim. Was she acting crazy today or what?...Did you hear her yell at me by the lockers? You did!...Richie was there, too?...You're kidding. Don't tell me! Do you think he heard? I'll die if he heard! Oh, I'm so embarrassed…I'm gonna kill her! It's a good thing she's one of my best friends or I swear I'd never speak to her again…Do you know who sent her that note she was trying to read in English today?…Did you see how many times she took it out?…I knew Carlson was gonna grab it for sure. Jeanna, DO YOU KNOW ANYTHING?"

Jeanna met Erica's racing monologue with a smattering of "yeahs" or "nos" intermingled with a perfunctory acceptance of Erica's apology. Jeanna then shared news that made Erica bolt upright, the heel of one sneaker tearing the ruffle on her new pink satin comforter as she planted her feet on the floor. "Mom's gonna kill me," she muttered, but there was no time to care. "What? What are you saying?"

"I'm saying that I think Kim's been avoiding us lately because she's in some kind of trouble…but I sure don't know how to help."

"Jeanna, what are you talking about? What kind of trouble?" Erica remembered her earlier panicked thought, the one that made her pen fly from her mouth. "She's not…she's not—"

"No, she's not!"

Erica slumped back with relief.

"And how could you even think that of Kim? If she knew you had even thought that, she'd never speak to you again! She's only been officially going out with Richie since April." Jeanna continuted indignantly. "Besides, you know Kim would never do anything like that, because we all agreed we never would until we are at least seniors. I can't believe you sometimes. Just be glad I'm not going to tell her you even thought that…and that's only because we're so close…"

Erica envisioned herself transporting through the phone line into Jeanna's messy room, squeezing her arm or yanking her dingy blonde hair until she stopped her lecture. "Jeanna, fine! Will you please shut up. I'm sorry…okay? It's just that I'm worried about Kim and I don't know what to think. Now will you please tell me what's going on?"

"Well, okay. I forgive you…but now listen to me and don't interrupt, because I know this is going to sound strange. I don't really understand it myself, so just listen." After a short pause Jeanna declared, "I think it has something to do with a diet."

Erica cupped her hand to her face, skinned it up her cheek, and through her thick black hair. She fought to contain the scream erupting inside her. "Are you out of your mind? I'm trying to figure out what's wrong with Kim, and you bring up a diet. Are you crazy? I practically hate you. If you weren't one of my best friends, I would…I would hate you."

The silence that followed gave Erica time to catch her breath, catch hold of her thoughts and the words she had just said. "I'm sorry, Jeanna," she whispered. "I didn't mean that. Honest. It's just that I've been trying to figure out what's wrong all afternoon, and I've been remembering stuff that I'm trying to make some sense of and I'm confused…and you're just making it worse."

After a breathy sigh Erica heard a welcomed, "It's okay. I forgive you again…I suppose." Unable to resist, Jeanna added, "But that's only because I'm so wonderful." Her tone quickly changed. "Okay, you said you were confused, Erica, so now just keep quiet and listen."

✷✷✷✷✷✷✷

When Erica hung up, the room was dark. She lay back slowly, absently reaching until she found her tattered bunny, Fred. She cradled his faded pink body against her shoulder. She turned and stared at a framed picture on her wall, now shadowed by early evening's veil. It was not so long ago that the newly formed threesome of friends had amused themselves by pretending to be the bunnies depicted in the tea party scene.

On a day Erica or one of her best friends felt particularly competent, she might declare herself Eva, the bunny pouring herself tea. Had one of the girls been approached by a boy at school, she might smugly claim the role of Marissa, the blushing bunny whose paw smothered a giggle as she listened to a perhaps naughty tale told by Shiloh, the only boy bunny in the entire scene. Happy or excited, each girl knew she would have to be Gladys, the bunny seated on the white wooden glider whose face squinted with delight from the taste of a half-eaten biscuit she held. Kim had played the game just as she and Jeanna had. No, not completely. Erica frowned with suspicion as she lay on her bed absently fingering Fred's threadbare head. Never—never would Kim claim to be Cynthia, the pudgy bunny (and the cutest, at least in the eyes of Jeanna and Erica) who offered a silver tray of white glazed biscuits to the party guests. Not even when she had done an appropriate polite or generous deed.

Erica's brow furrowed as she propped herself up with her forearm. Kim has always refused to be Cynthia, the pudgy rabbit. If Jeanna is right and Kim is in some secret diet club, then…Silently and urgently Erica prodded her mind: Then what? But nothing would come. What was the connection? Was there a connection?

Erica thought about Kim's ever present obsession with weight, in spite of the fact that she was perfect, not even close to fat. None of us are, Erica vacantly reassured herself for the second time that day. And she was not unaware that it was the second time. Of all her friends Kim was not the one who needed to lose weight. Kim was thin! Yet she dieted like everybody else. And everybody diets. Oh no. Erica slumped back heavily. The words catapulted her to a memory she would have preferred permanently erased.

Two on. Two out. Erica on third. The last softball game of the season. Tied score. Jeanna had bunted as Erica lunged for home. Amidst shouts of "Slide, Erica, slide!" she heard Kim yell: "Slide! Slide, fatty, slide!" The microsecond Erica had used to absorb the insult did not stop her from hearing what she had really needed to hear: "Safe!"

Kim's jeer had devastated Erica, had robbed her of her greatest moment. She grimaced, recalling her shame and anger as she forced an empty smile for the victory photo. "Why did you call me fatty?" Erica remembered asking, and the painful echo of Kim's giggle was immediate: "Oh, I was just kidding."

Was she? Was Kim kidding? Am I fat? No. Erica asked and answered her questions now as she had done then. She recalled the comfort of Jeanna's oath on their friendship that if Erica did have to lose weight, it was eleven—"No, not fifteen!"—pounds at the most. And she recalled her mother's betrayal later on that day, when she called Erica's extra weight "nothing more than baby fat" that would disappear with more exercise. Erica stirred. How did her mother not realize that her intended solace including her suggestions that Erica cut out fats and junk food had actually confirmed Kim's indictment?

The unwelcomed scene and its incriminating aftermath played itself through as Erica heard Kim's final words, the words that had pried open its curtain: "...Besides, Erica, it's no big deal...Everybody can afford to lose a few pounds, even me. Just go on a diet. Everybody diets."

Once in a while Erica had, indeed, thought about the diet that would eventually snare her. She called it her *driver's license* diet and knew it was inevitable. She could not bear the thought of carrying around a piece of plastic that would so brutally define her: one hundred forty pounds; five feet, four inches; (boring) brown hair and eyes. Erica wished she trusted someone enough to ask whether the motor vehicle department employed people who actually weighed and measured you. Maybe they simply expected people to complete the application honestly. But whom could she ask without revealing so much, too much, about herself? Ugh.

With a forced head shake Erica erased the past, stared at her ceiling, and listed the facts anew. One: Kim did not need to lose weight. Erica conceded that she, of all her friends, might actually need to lose (just) a few pounds. (And hadn't she even lost a few baby fat pounds since that awful incident?) Whatever. It was certainly not Kim who needed to lose weight. Two: According to Jeanna, Kim was, in fact, dieting. Three: Jeanna suspected a secret diet club as the possible source of Kim's problem. The facts coupled with her memories were like jigsaw puzzle pieces without a picture showing how the pieces might connect or what, when connected, they might portray.

In the hushed stillness of her room, Erica absently curled Fred's floppy ear around her fingers and once again studied the picture above her desk. She wondered why she had never seriously questioned Kim's refusal to be Cynthia, the hostess, the star of the print, *Cynthia's Tea Party*. "We should have asked her!" Erica huskily whispered into Fred's ragged ear. We should have put it right to her: How come you never want to be Cynthia?...I know it sounds dumb. I know it was pretend and we were just kids...but maybe I'd understand more...now. Erica blew out a frustrated breath: "We gotta do something."

"Erica? Philip? I'm home!"

Erica closed her eyes and smiled as she heard the front door close. Mom's home. She quickly changed from her "good" jeans and white rayon blouse to her "junk" jeans and oversized sweatshirt. Loping down the stairs Erica slowed her pace when she heard Philip retelling his good news. Her news about Kim—and the torn ruffle—would have to wait. Maybe she'd say nothing about the tear and try mending it herself. After all, Life Skills and Management had begun with a sewing unit that had to be good for something.

"Hi, Mom," Erica said flatly entering the kitchen just as Philip was finishing his report: "...and then Erica hung it up right there so you could see it."

"Oh, hi, honey. Philip's had some day, huh? He's been telling me..." Erica's mother stopped when she noticed her daughter's frown. "What's wrong, Erica? Bad day?"

"You might say that."

Gail heard the need in Erica's tone and wanted to meet it but there Philip stood expectantly. She picked him up anchoring his bottom with her forearm. "I am very proud of you for getting so many stars for your project." Suddenly embarrassed, Philip patted his mother's cheeks nervously. "And I'm going to keep that poster right where it is. As a matter of fact," Gail added as she nodded her head toward his work, "all those neat pictures can help me plan our dinners."

Philip's eyes squinted with doubt then widened with half-belief. He finally smiled and wrapped his arms around his mother's neck.

"Whose big boy are you?"

"Yours, Mommy!"

"Good," Gail said as she eased him down. "Now you go play while I get dinner ready. I want to talk with Erica about her day."

"Can I play with Diamond?"

"Of course. Where is that cat anyway?"

"I know, I know! He's in my room."

The women watched Philip race from the kitchen, each envious (for different reasons) of his youth. Erica faced her mother and tried to sound cheerful. "So how was your day, Mom?"

"My day was fine. Never mind my day. How was your day? You don't look good at all. Did something happen?"

"Oh Mom," Erica pleaded. "I don't know what to do!"

Erica's dramatic tone alerted her mother's suspicion. "Okay, Erica," Gail almost droned. "What's the matter?"

"Kim's been on this diet and me and Jeanna—"

"Jeanna and I," Gail interrupted.

"Oh, Mom," Erica groaned but obliged her mother. "Jeanna and *I*...didn't really know anything about it at first and even if we did, it wouldn't have mattered because we're all always on diets, kind of, especially Kim, and so we didn't think anything of it because we just figured she was trying a different diet, but then Richie—"

"Stop." Gail pressed her palms down in mid-air. "I really want to listen, Erica, but you're rambling. Think about what you're trying to say before you say it so I can understand you."

Erica had heard this warning before. Rolling her eyes, she sat on a stool by the counter where her mother had just placed a wooden bowl. She folded her hands, thumbs tapping, and once again accommodated her mother. "Richie...wrote a note...to Kim."

"Okay, wait." Gail squinted her eyes toward the ceiling then darted them back at Erica as she snapped one finger to a point: "Richie's going out with Kim now, right?" Erica nodded impatiently as her mother beamed with self-satisfaction. "Okay, I got it. Kim's on a diet. Richie wrote a note. So what was in the note? And please, don't ramble."

Her mother had again cautioned her to think and speak slowly while Erica really needed to race, stammer, and forget about grammar!

"Richie told Jeanna that he wrote a note to Kim warning her he would break up with her if she didn't quit her crazy diet..."

"What diet?"

"Exactly. That's what I've been trying to tell you. We didn't know about any diet until now. I mean I did notice Kim lost a few pounds lately, but she's always trying to look like Kate Moss anyway so it was no big deal. But then Jeanna said Richie found out that Kim and these two other girls made a bet to see who could get down to eighty-five pounds because they think—"

"What girls are you talking about?" Gail had taken several pieces of cooked chicken from the refrigerator and was cutting them into small cubes when she looked up from the cutting board and added, "And Erica, please slow down."

With deliberate control and a silent *gawd!* Erica explained: "Jenell and Amy, two girls. It doesn't matter, Mom...you don't know them...they're not real close friends, just friends. Anyway, they made this bet...or pact...club...whatever it is with Kim. I only just now heard about all this from Jeanna. Can you believe that? I'm her best friend, too. Anyway, they want to get down to eighty-five pounds by Christmas so that even if they pig out over the holidays, they'll be way under one hundred pounds.

"That's ridiculous."

"Yeah, I know. Anyway, Jeanna told me that Richie overheard Amy bragging about it to one of his friends and he got really mad so he went to Kim and told her he thought her diet club was stupid, but she refused to talk to him, so he wrote her a note telling her in plain English how crazy he thought it was...and that she should quit her stupid diet."

"Well, good for him," Gail declared rapping the counter with the knife handle.

"Yeah, well, he gave her an ultimatum in that note of his. He warned her that if she didn't stop trying to get down to eighty-five pounds, he would break up with her."

"Eighty-five pounds," Gail mumbled as she swept a hair from her eye with the back of her hand. "Kim shouldn't even weigh less than a hundred pounds. She's at least five-three, five-four, isn't she? I've never heard a stupider thing in all my life."

"You're right, mom. She's five-three. And, Mom," Erica added with a grin, "is *stupider* a word?"

"Hmmm...Well, I'm not sure now that you ask." Gail smiled, glad her daughter's spirits were lifting, even if it was at her expense. She made a mental note to look "stupid" up in a dictionary. "Do their mothers know about all this?" she asked as she folded chunks of pineapple, cashews, and celery into the chicken.

"Their mothers? Maw'm," Erica whined. "It's a diet. Everybody diets!" She cringed, astonished she had used the very phrase that had leveled her earlier. She unclasped her hands and planted them on the counter. Why am I defending Kim? Eighty-five pounds is a bit much. "Mom, I only just found out myself...and do you really think any of them would tell their mothers? Jeanna and me...I...just can't believe Kim was a part of something like this and didn't even tell us. Why didn't she tell us? We're her best friends!" Leaning heavily on the counter, Erica furrowed her brow and rubbed its wrinkles hard. "I feel like I let her down."

Gail smirked. "Oh, Erica, what could you have done? If she wants to try a crazy diet, for heaven's sake."

"Well, I kinda sensed something was weird right from the first day school started," Erica said more to herself than out loud, "only I never told anyone. I figured it was because she'd just come back from her dad's. She always comes back weird and moody when she's been with him. It takes her a few weeks to de-program."

"De-program?" Gail asked as she poured honey lemon dressing onto the chicken salad.

"Yeah, that's what we call it when she comes back from her visits to her father's house." Gail stopped pouring just for a moment, long enough for Erica to catch the frown her mother immediately tried to hide with a slight turn of her head.

Stupid. Erica filled the uncomfortable moment by walking to the refrigerator. She poured herself a glass of milk, knowing she had picked up the whole milk and not the two percent container. She stared into the glass as she drank, cursing herself for mentioning fathers. She politely avoided her mother's eyes while they probably stole glimpses of a happier time before her father and her grandmother had become victims of a drunk driver.

A cellophane sheet zipped across a cutting-edge, ending the awkward moment. Gail covered her cashew chicken salad with the plastic wrap and opened the refrigerator door. "Well, de-bugged, de-programmed, whatever you call it." Gail managed a natural tone, speaking as though no time had passed. "Do you have any idea what you're going to do with this information? It could be serious, you know."

Erica set her glass on the counter hard and waved her hands wildly. "I do know! You should have heard her today. She nearly snapped my head off. I thought maybe after I finished telling you what happened, *you'd* have some ideas."

Gail raised her eyebrows and half-smiled. "Well thanks for the vote of confidence." She slid the bowl onto a shelf, paused to take in the cool air, then finally closed the refrigerator door. "But to be honest with you, I haven't a clue and I'm starving. Let me get into some comfortable clothes and we'll talk about it at dinner. Deal?"

"Deal."

III
Bus Stop

Erica bolted out of bed the moment her alarm buzzed, a first. She raced through her usually lengthy bathroom ritual and threw together a quick outfit, another first. She thundered down the stairs to the kitchen and poured herself a too-full bowl of corn flakes. Her crunching echoed through her head along with her thoughts. No matter how hard she tried to figure things out on her own, it was always easier when her mother helped. She knew so many girls who didn't get along with their mothers, actually hated them. Would she ever be like that? Mom's not perfect, she thought, but who is? She decided if she didn't hate her mother by now, she probably never would.

Erica shoveled a heaping spoonful of the harder to find still crisp corn flakes into her mouth. She loved cereal and it didn't matter what kind although she preferred the sugary ones she tried to avoid. Erica knew a lot of girls who routinely skipped breakfast. She paused playing her spoon against a few soggy flakes before sighing then digging her spoon into the bowl for another mouthful.

She paused mid-chew when she remembered how sad her mother had gotten the evening before when she had regretfully mentioned fathers. Erica was only twelve when a drunk driver had killed her father and grandmother. A treasured life support system of photographs kept Erica's memories of them alive. Recalling their deaths had caused one of those moments that made her feel sad, trapped, and alone. She swallowed hard.

"Hi, Eri."

Philip's arrival was a welcomed distraction. "Hi, honey bunch. What would you like for breakfast?"

"Same as you," Philip answered predictably. Erica got up to prepare Philip's breakfast and though her back was to him while she filled his bowl, she quietly mouthed the line she knew was coming.

"Is Mommy up yet?"

She grinned. "Yeah, I heard her in the shower." Her satisfaction was brief. She suddenly wondered how much Philip remembered about their father. He was barely three when he died. She carefully poured milk onto the corn flakes in his Batman bowl and breathed heavily, wishing she could make things different for them all.

Forcing a smile, she returned to the kitchen table. "Here ya' go, sport." She debated whether or not she should sit with him. Ordinarily, she remained with Philip until their mother arrived; but today she wanted to get to the bus stop as soon as possible so she could talk with Jeanna about creating a plan that would help Kim. Leaving her almost empty cereal bowl on the table, she kissed Philip on the cheek warmly, grabbed her books and bag and raced out the door. "Bye, mom!" she yelled to the upstairs hallway. "I promise to clean the kitchen when I get home. Promise!"

❋❋❋❋❋❋❋

The first person Erica hurried to at the crowded bus stop was Steve, Richie's best friend. She hoped not to share her information with him, but to squeeze information from him, if he had any. Last night her mother had suggested that one of the best ways to help Kim would be to learn as much as there was to learn about Kim's problem, no, *situation*. Understanding the situation more fully might ease Erica's sense of helplessness and alarm. The suggestion made sense to Erica, who planned to follow the advice, then calmly arrange a meeting with Kim for a friendly discussion. It sounded simple.

"Yo, Erica. What's up?"

"Hi, Steve. Nothin' much." Okay, how do I pry information out of him? I'm no detective. No time passed before Steve himself offered the wedge: "D'ya hear I might not make the wrestling team?"

"No way!"

"Way. Coach Hawks says if I don't lose the six pounds I put on over the summer, I'm out when the season starts, and he doesn't care what kind of record I had in junior high."

"But, Steve, you got taller this summer." Erica momentarily forgot about Kim. "Doesn't that count for something?"

"For something, yeah, but not much," Steve said flatly. I'm too light to make the next division, and I'm too heavy for mine. I've been starving myself and running everyday but I'm just not losing an ounce."

Erica stared at Steve helplessly not knowing what to say. This is nuts. Dieting is making all my friends crazy. She touched his forearm gently when suddenly

Steve ended the awkward moment: "Hey, Kim was mighty pissed at you yesterday."

Clutching her book bag to her chest, Erica spun around and squealed, "Oh, gawd, were you there to hear it?" She glared at several girls who stood nearby giggling.

"Yeah. No big deal. She's been grouchy to everyone lately. Why should you be left out?" Steve periodically shifted his hands from his back to front pockets and his weight from one foot to the other as if working through a private practice drill. "What's up with her, anyway?"

"I'm not sure," she almost whispered. *Should I tell him what I know?*

"I figure she's a little crazy 'cause of that diet she's on."

He knows about the diet!

"And if that's it, man..." He shifted his weight once again, "I sure can relate." He glanced down the street and said, "Hey, here comes the bus." Spotting Jeanna frantically rushing toward them, he yelled, "Yo', Jeanna, ya' better move it. You're gonna miss your ride to Paradise!"

Erica stood fast with Steve, holding their places in the front of the line, focused for the moment on securing their regular seats in the rear of bus. Once seated she waited impatiently for Jeanna, who was stalled by the slow moving bodies in front of her. Erica smiled approvingly when a senior barked at the girls who had giggled at her earlier: "It's not like it matters where you sit, fa' gawd's sake. Sit anywhere!"

When Jeanna finally reached Erica, she plopped into the seat, threw her head on Erica's shoulder and moaned, "What are we going to do about Kim?"

"Don't worry." Erica heard her mother in her own voice. She was somewhat satisfied by the effect. "We'll figure out something," Erica added patting her hand lightly on Jeanna's knee. "I've got this whole thing figured out." What she had figured out was really very sketchy. Where she was going with it was sketchier still. But someone had to do something!

IV

Taking Charge

Lunch time noise filled the cafeteria. Erica craned her neck and stretched on tiptoe while carefully balancing her tray. Yes, Kim was at her usual table in the far back corner with Amy and Jenell. When school had begun weeks ago, Kim had announced to Erica that she would be having lunch with Amy and Jenell, girls like her who could relate to divorce, girls she needed to talk to. Erica regretted how willingly she had believed the excuse. Surely these were Kim's fellow members in the secret diet club.

Without hesitation that would make her think twice, maybe even retreat, Erica marched toward them. "Hey, guys, what's up?" Erica forced a light tone to catch the girls off guard. It worked.

"Nothing much," Amy said. "Sit down if ya' want. There's room."

Slowly lowering her eyelids, Kim raised her chin and turned away. Ignoring the deliberate snub, Erica noted that none of them had a lunch tray, although Jenell was holding a container of low fat chocolate milk, a fingernail methodically peeling the wax off its surface. Erica planned to follow her mother's advice. Take the situation in hand calmly and directly. Learn as much as you can. But how can I talk to Kim with Amy and Jenell sitting here? Take a deep breath, Erica.

Here it goes. "If you girls wouldn't mind, I really need to talk with Kim about something. I won't be long. Promise." Unable to resist she added, "Anyway, it looks like you're all through with your lunches."

Catching Erica's tone if not her intent, both girls glared at Erica, who matched their glares with one of her own and pleased herself by adding a defiant smile. Almost simultaneously they yielded: "Fine" and left the table.

"Catch you later," Kim called out to them hopefully. "So," her friendly tone now hostile, "what do you want to talk to me about?"

Slowly, calmly, Erica began: Kim's note and her rudeness at the locker yesterday; Jeanna's conversation with Richie; knowledge of the secret diet club. She ended with a compassionate plea: "I want to help you in any way I can because you're my friend, but I need to know more to understand."

Kim's steel blue eyes narrowed and her knuckles whitened. "Well, aren't you too good, Erica," she sneered. "Maybe you should start a Little Miss Helpful column in the school newspaper. Or should that be Little Miss Nosy?"

Speechless, Erica slouched back. The light-hearted tone with which Kim delivered her words had successfully intensified their cruelty.

"If butting in where you're not welcome is your idea of friendship," Kim continued, "then maybe we shouldn't be friends anymore. Maybe we've outgrown each other. Maybe—"

"Maybe, Kim…" Erica interrupted with a strength she could not identify, "you should cut this tough act garbage. Just tell me if it's true that the weight you've lost these past couple of weeks is because of some idiotic plan to starve yourself." She left Kim no time to reply. "Because if it is, and you're not going to listen to me and realize how stupid and dangerous your plan is—" *What do I say now? What do I say now?* "I'll find someone you'll have to listen to!" Erica immediately regretted her threat, angry her mother had not given her more explicit instructions.

No longer smirking, Kim bolted from her chair. "You talk to anybody about this and you're dead to me." She continued her assault quietly, clipping each word. "I won't look at you. I won't speak to you. Ever again. It's a diet. Just a diet, dammit!" Distracted by a sudden flurry of turning heads, Kim sat down but not before darting her angry eyes at the unwelcomed spectators. "How I diet, who I diet with, and why I diet is none of your damn business! I'm fat. I hate being fat!" she almost cried. "I want to lose a little weight. Big deal. And I don't care what Richie said to you…"

Erica's stomach tingled. *Fat?* Kim's irrational self-indictment frightened Erica even more than the raspy whisper Kim used to deliver the charge, but there was no time for questions now. "No! Richie didn't say anything to me, not to me, I swear he didn't," Erica pleaded. "Richie told Jeanna—"

"Ah, yes…Jeanna." Kim tapped her fingers rapidly against her collarbone as she conjured her final blow. "Richie had no right telling Jeanna anything about that note. And if he wants to break up with me because I want to look good, let him. He should look in the mirror sometimes. So should you. He can drop dead for all I care. So can you!" Kim clenched her teeth to control her wavering tone. "Where do you get off making what I do with my life your business anyway? Who needs your help, Erica? Leave me alone. I'm not your brother or your mother. *I* don't need you!" Within seconds Kim's enraged face had donned a veil of a cool indifference.

Erica was stunned. The episode shook her more than her fourteen years could comprehend. She had not expected a verbal lashing although she had expected Kim to be a little angry. But this was not about anger. This was something much more than anger. Erica forced herself to stand. She rubbed her neck to ease the painful lump filling her throat, not caring how foolish she knew she must appear. Before she turned and rushed away, she cried to herself: Who is this person?

V

Dying to be Thin

Gail arrived home later than usual. She found Erica asleep on the sofa with Diamond purring contentedly on her stomach. Philip sat by Erica's feet turning the pages of a picture book. "Sshh," he whispered, "Erica doesn't feel good."

Gail hurried toward them and smooched Philip's expectant lips. She sat down beside Erica and touched her forehead with the back of her fingers. Erica inhaled deeply and instinctively restrained Diamond from bolting. She opened her eyes to see whose body sat so closely. "Oh, Mom," she mumbled then, "Oh, Mom!" Erica freed the yowling cat who immediately padded away. She reached up and hugged her mother tightly. "Oh, Mom, something awful happened today."

"What, Erica? What?" Gail rubbed the back of her daughter's head and rocked her gently.

"Kim's got a problem all right," she moaned, "but it's a lot bigger than a diet and I don't have any idea what it is! I'm so scared. She acted crazy today. I didn't even get a chance to ask her anything. She said such awful things to me. All in this weird kind of whisper growl, I don't know, like she wanted to threaten me or something. I can't even explain it. And, Mom," Erica gasped: "Kim thinks she's fat!"

Gail stroked Erica's disheveled hair and turned to see that Philip had closed his book and was watching them anxiously. "Philip, honey, will you please leave the room so that Erica and I can have some girl talk?" Philip nodded slowly and inched his bottom off the sofa. He headed toward the kitchen mumbling, and Erica looked at her brother guiltily. "Mom, it's okay, I'm all right. Philip doesn't have to leave." Philip stopped and turned expectantly.

"Erica, don't be absurd!" Gail protested. "You go on now, Philip, and thank you."

"We're going out to eat tonight, Mommy, right, 'cause it's Friday."

"Yes, honey, and you can be in charge of where we eat tonight."

Philip skipped in a circle. "Burger King, Burger King, Burger King!"

Eager to hasten his exit, Gail agreed. "Burger King it is." She watched Philip skip out of the living room singing about having it his way. Her eyes narrowed when she heard Erica apologetically call out after him: "I'll read to you before we leave, Philip. Promise." Gail sighed. She wondered whether Erica's excessive concern for her brother was any worse than good old fashioned sibling rivalry.

After the few minutes in which Erica related what had happened, Gail assured her daughter everything would be all right (although she was not at all sure). "It sounds like Kim does have a real problem. But maybe...maybe there's a way we can at least try to help." Erica slouched back and looked at her mother skeptically. Gail stood up and smoothed the front of her skirt. "Erica, come on upstairs with me. I want to talk with you some more while we get ready for Friday night burgers. And I want to call someone I know who might be able to give us some advice.

✼✼✼✼✼✼✼

To Erica the biggest payoff from her steady baby-sitting job was the luxury it afforded her: her very own private telephone line. She dialed Jeanna and barely waited for her hello. "You're not going to believe what my mom's doing. Right now, right while I'm talking with you."

"Having dinner with Brad Pitt."

"No, jerk. Besides, we're going out for dinner and he wasn't invited. Be serious, Jeanna. She's calling Marilyn Grayson."

"Wow, Erica, that's just great," she said sarcastically then immediately snapped, "What the heck do I care? Who's Marilyn Grayson?...Boy, you sure made a speedy recovery. Are you the same person who told me on the bus today that she never had a worse day in her whole life? What about that tongue lashing you got from Kim at lunch? You sure mend easy."

Erica waited patiently for Jeanna's teasing to end. She was too excited to care. She waited until she heard nothing but the static of her portable phone. "No, dummy. I don't mend easy. That's just it. I was so upset I told my mom everything and she's gonna help. She's calling her friend, well, not really a friend, but it's someone who she knows real well from the building where she works...Marilyn Grayson...she's a shrink. Well, not exactly a shrink. She's a psychotherapist." Erica interpreted Jeanna's silence as her sarcastic way of saying a big fat "SO?" Then Jeanna actually said it. "SO?!"

"So guess what kind of patients she specializes in?"

"Do tell." Jeanna was unyielding.

"People with eating disorders."

This new silence delighted Erica. She was certain that this time Jeanna was impressed.

The phone conversation lasted twenty minutes. She paused only once to answer her jiggling doorknob: "Philip, I promise, honest. I'll be off the phone real soon and then I'll read to you. Yes…I know I said before dinner and I will. I promise!"

✸✸✸✸✸✸✸

Erica scraped hangars left and right across her closet's bar searching for the oversized pullover sweater she liked to wear to Friday night dinners. But her thoughts distracted her. All Erica had really known about eating disorders was what she had learned in health class. She knew the difference between bulimia and anorexia, even got a good grade on last year's unit test. Almost everyone she knew dieted once in a while, pigged out, then fasted to balance things out. It had never mattered. She even knew some girls who blew it if they felt like they really ate too much, convinced that fasting took too long. Disgusting, she thought. But she genuinely had never considered any of their behavior even remotely related to real eating disorders. Dieting, even gross dieting, was just the way it was. (Whether she liked it or not!) Eating disorders had nothing to do with it. Until now. She found the sweater neatly folded over a hangar and groaned patiently: "Maw'm."

Erica walked to her mother's bedroom door and opened it. "Can I come in, Mom?" she asked hesitantly.

"Sure. I'm almost ready," Gail mumbled while leaning toward her dresser's mirror fingering clear gloss on her lower lip.

"Oh that's okay. I still have to read to Philip. But..." she hesitated, "I was just wondering about your phone call."

"Yes. I know. Well, the bad news is Marilyn agrees that Kim may have a problem. The good news, or at least the not-so-bad news is..." Gail directed her eyes and a smile toward Erica who looked at her mother's reflection expectantly: "Marilyn said she'll help us if she can."

VI
Losing Friends

Monday morning Mrs. Bouton directed the class to read the review chapter on lifestyle choices and answer the questions at the end of the unit. Ordinarily Erica moaned over such a boring assignment. Was anybody duller than Bouton? Today, however, Erica welcomed the silent reading time. She had just passed a letter to Kim and the boring activity would give Kim ample time to read it, maybe even write back. Erica had written the letter after a weekend of extensive research. Marilyn Grayson, concerned about Kim after what she had heard, personally delivered pamphlets and books to the Shepherd's house for Erica to read. Disappointed that she had taken Philip to the park and had missed the visit, Erica felt happy, too. The therapist had stayed and talked with her mother for more than an hour. "We talked and talked about so many things," her mother had said. Erica hoped they talked about other things besides Kim. Being a young widow with two kids had to be awful hard.

After devouring every page that Marilyn had provided, Erica was certain she could have written a term paper as well as the three page letter she had just passed to Kim. Her research had even made her question her frequent paraphrasing of Shakespeare: *to eat or not to eat it, that is the question.* Might she have an eating disorder, too? She dismissed the unsettling thought, not just because she knew only too well she typically opted to eat rather than not, but because right now she was far too worried about Kim. She hoped that Kim would be pleased by her hefty note filled with concern and helpful information, like the fact that some teenagers, rather than deal with pain—like the kind that comes from divorce—fall prey to eating disorders. Erica was confident her letter would make Kim realize how much she wanted to help. Maybe Kim would even apologize!

Erica checked her watch; eight minutes had passed. She looked up from her text book and slowly turned. Kim crushed Erica's tenuous smile with her waiting sneer. She carefully refolded the pages into their original triangular shape. Erica realized Kim had waited for an audience of one to stage her show: She got up, blinked her eyes dully at Erica as she passed and flicked the note into the waste basket by Mrs. Bouton's desk.

"Kim," Mrs. Bouton chided, "you know you're supposed to wait until the end of class for that sort of thing."

"Oh, yes, Mrs. Bouton, I'm sorry," Kim replied too sweetly. She darted a smirk at Erica adding, "I guess I forgot."

****

Erica's day was a total waste. If something had been taught she had no clue what it might be. Kim had severed their relationship with a silent act and a steely look that Erica was sure should be used by and for adults only. She was hurt beyond tears, beyond anger, certainly beyond telling anyone about it. How many of her friends had asked her: "What's wrong with you today?" How many had impatiently shrugged her off when she failed to respond?

She sat on the bus staring out the window, having lost one of her best friends and alienated more including Jeanna who sat sullenly beside her. Erica longed for her father. She retreated to a long ago time when she and Kim had seriously argued.

They had just become seventh graders and Erica had looked to her father for comfort rather than her mother. Kim's father had threatened to move out of his house. All men were horrible Kim had cried, vowing she would never ever get married. Erica had sat with her head on her father's shoulder demanding without words his promise that he never leave her mother, his children. He had answered her need with reassuring words of fidelity. She savored the musky scent of his after shave that she could almost smell, even now. She remembered the feel of his strong fingers stroking her cheek as he spoke. A month later, he was dead. The lump that swelled in her throat was impossible to eliminate and now just added to her pain.

VII

The Plan

After eating two slices of twelve grain bread smeared with thick layers of crunchy peanut butter drizzled with clover honey Erica was ready to talk to someone. She naturally chose Jeanna. Upon calling, however, she almost immediately wished she had waited for her mother to get home instead. "I can't just go over there, Erica! Kim knows that everything you know, I know. She'll treat me like she did you today and no, thank you very much, I'll pass."

Erica squeezed the phone to her ear with her left shoulder as she mended the comforter she had torn days earlier. She stopped mid-stitch to say, "Jeanna, you need to look at the situation realistically. You are our only hope. I can't go to Kim now. Haven't I explained enough for you to know that by now? Stop being so selfish. Think about our friend. She needs help and right now…well…she hates me, or at least she thinks she hates me. If you go over to her house and act like nothing's happened, maybe you can see how things are over there…if anything seems strange…what it's like with her mother…if her mother even knows."

"No way. Her mother's so—"

"Jeanna, her mother is nice." Erica safely completed the sentence.

"But she's always there. She's so…oppressive!"

"She is not. She just worries about Kim, that's all. You don't know what it's like for Mrs. Spencer. Kim is all she has." She was tired of pleading. "Look, Jeanna. Are you or are you not my friend and Kim's friend?" Silence. "Jeanna?"

"Fine," Jeanna conceded softly. "We're friends."

"Good. Then it's settled." Only then did Erica continue to mend the tear realizing she should have used a lighter thread. "You'll go over to Kim's house. You'll act casual. Just observe things. Maybe even stay for dinner. You know Mrs. Spencer will ask you. And you must say yes."

"Why?"

"Isn't it obvious? For one, you'll learn whether Kim eats dinner at all and two…as a result of one…whether her mother is even aware that Kim is on a deadly diet."

"Deadly?"

"Ouch!" Erica sucked on the finger she had just stuck with the needle. "Well, Jeanna, Kim's trying to lose over twenty pounds when she doesn't even need to lose one. What would you like to call it?"

✻✻✻✻✻✻✻

Jeanna lifted the shiny brass clapper, hesitated, then knocked it forcefully three times. Erica had advised her not to call beforehand and of course she hadn't; Kim certainly wouldn't have agreed to a visit. The door opened. "Well, hello, Jeanna! How are you? I haven't seen you in ages. Come on in!" Caught off guard by the flurry of words, Jeanna cringed under

Mrs. Spencer's unexpected embrace but forced herself to relax. "Kim's upstairs...Kim, Jeanna's here," she shouted brightly into the air.

Mrs. Spencer whisked Jeanna through the hallway toward Kim's room. "How's school, Jeanna? Do you like your new teachers? I think Kim is pleased with all of hers although she hasn't really told me much. I'll just have to wait for teacher conference night to find out for myself."

Jeanna interjected brief, polite responses: "Fine...Fine...Yes...Good idea." Surprisingly she welcomed Mrs. Spencer's incessant chatter; it delayed the inevitable, the unknown. Jeanna privately regretted she had come, vowing Erica would pay her back, big time, for this favor.

Mrs. Spencer tapped on Kim's door lightly before opening it. "Kim, it's Jeanna...Good grief! Turn down that racket! I can hear it through your headphones. You'll be deaf before you're twenty. Jeanna, do you listen to music that loud?"

Jeanna gave, rather than a truthful response, at least a neutral one: "I think I do sometimes, Mrs. Spencer." She dared not annoy Kim who lay on her bed smirking.

"You see, Kim?" Mrs. Spencer said, deciding Jeanna had agreed.

"Fine, Mom," Kim said curtly before shifting to a syrupy voice. "Hello, Jeanna. How sweet of you to come." Kim clicked the off button with her middle finger rigid. Kim's gesture was totally lost on her mother, but not Jeanna, who stood awkwardly at the door until she mustered a nonchalant: "I was bored, so I thought I'd come over and hang out for a while. What's up?"

Mrs. Spencer turned to leave. "I'll bring you two a snack and some drinks—"

"No, Mom, don't bring anything."

Kim's mother turned abruptly. "Kim, what's wrong with you and where are your manners? This is the first time you've had one of your friends over in ages. You know I always—"

"I know you always!" Kim shouted and catching herself exerted a polite retreat. "But you shouldn't have to. We're old enough, Mom. If we want something, we'll get it ourselves."

Mrs. Spencer pondered the statement and, though not completely satisfied, turned to leave the room. "Okay, but if you want something—"

"Maw'm," Kim whined.

"Okay, okay," Mrs. Spencer smiled. "Well, you two have a nice visit."

Jeanna drew in a breath and exhaled. "So Kim, what's up?"

"Nothin' much," Kim answered guardedly. "How about you?"

"Nothing much…What were you doing?" By now Jeanna was lying on the queen sized bed facing Kim, her head propped by an opened palm just like Kim's. Be careful. Don't blow this, she thought. So far so good.

"Nothing really…just listening to music…and writing."

Kim's downward glance directed Jeanna to the lavender book that lay between them. "Hey, you have a diary just like Erica's…"*Oh no! Why did I mention Erica?*

Jeanna was relieved when Kim ignored the slip and leaned slightly to reach the book. "Yeah, we both got them for each other last year for Christmas. Don't you remember? You said you hated to write so we got you a calendar with puppies on it...and the stuffed poodle," Kim swooned, "you absolutely had to have!"

Jeanna giggled. "Yeah, I remember." Here was the Kim that she knew. Oh, if only Erica could be here, she thought. She's blowin' this whole diet thing way out of proportion. Jeanna now had no idea why she had come, or what she would or should do next. She had no plan. No strategy. Darn that Erica. She decided she would hang out for a while then leave: mission aborted.

VIII
The Theft

If anyone had ever told Jeanna she would one day become a thief, she would have been insulted and hurt. But then the phone rang, Mrs. Spencer yelled to Kim to answer it, Kim rushed from her bed dropping the diary to the floor, and Jeanna did, in fact, become a thief.

Not exactly. At first she had just stared hungrily at the lavender book lying on the white carpet. What I wouldn't give to read Kim's diary she had thought. Maybe I could find out some valuable information. At first it was just an innocent temptation. But less than a minute after Kim had left her room Jeanna succumbed to that temptation.

She rolled herself diagonally across and off the bed breaking her fall with the grace of her ten years of gymnastics. She grabbed the book to steal a glimpse when, too suddenly, she heard Kim's returning footsteps. In less time than it took her to gasp, Jeanna spotted her black leather sack lying on the floor beside her and shoved the book into it between mirror, brush, wallet, and makeup pouch. The sound of the zipper closing filled her with an exhilarating rush of terror.

By the time Kim opened the door, Jeanna was standing by Kim's book shelves blowing invisible dust off the box she held. Feigning surprise she turned and asked lightly, "What say we have a go at *Jenga*, Kim?" Jeanna's heart pounded.

****

The game meant to distract Kim was successful—and to Jeanna—endless. Jeanna felt as though the diary was a caged alien that might at any moment burst through its leather prison. Though very thirsty and, although she hated to admit it, hungry, she asked for nothing. Why, the mere mention of drink or food to Kim, and the whole mission could blow up in her face.

Yes, come to think of it, it was a mission after all. Wouldn't Erica be pleased to learn that her timid little friend, Jeanna, had secured a source of information that surely held the answers to their questions. There was no need to justify *how* she obtained the book.

Jeanna rode her bike to Erica's house leisurely. She swung her sack by its shoulder strap forward then back, creating an arc just shy of a complete circle.

IX
The Diary

"You what?"

"I…"

"Tell me I didn't hear you right. Tell me I thought I heard that you took her diary, but that I was just having a dream…no…a nightmare. Tell me I didn't hear right."

In the seconds that lapsed between Jeanna's announcement and Erica's first shout, Diamond, who had been sleeping in Erica's room, awoke, jumped from Erica's bed, his tail full, underbelly hugging the carpet. When Jeanna yelled, "You heard right and I did!" the cat bounded from the room.

Erica closed her door, sighed deeply and turned around. "I don't believe it. I don't believe it…" The repeated phrase enraged Jeanna.

"Well, believe it because I did it! Who do you think you are anyway? You told me to go there…so I went! Did you tell me what to do? No…Act casual," Jeanna sneered. "Observe things…see what you can find out." Jeanna paced, flailing her arms and hands wildly as though she were a lawyer presenting an impassioned closing argument. "A lot of help you were!" Jeanna postured herself defiantly in front of Erica, her index finger pointing definitively toward her feet. "When Kim left that room, I did the first thing that came to my head!"

A heavy silence filled the room until Erica finally spoke. "I'm sorry, Jeanna." Erica extended her arms hesitantly. Jeanna, somewhat relieved, accepted Erica's hug. "This is all my fault," she whispered. "I shouldn't have asked you to go to Kim's...I know you didn't mean to steal it," she said sympathetically.

Jeanna pushed away roughly. "I didn't steal it!" She began to cry and rushed to Erica's bed, covering her tear-filled face in a pillow she wrenched from beneath the comforter. She lifted her head long enough to add: "I didn't mean to take her diary. I only wanted to peek. I got scared when I heard Kim coming back and I panicked...Okay?...I just wanted to help. You said I should help! You said I was being selfish." Jeanna wept into the pillow. Muffled sobs disturbed the silent minute that followed. Erica watched expectantly as Jeanna finally sat up, wiped her face in her shirt sleeve and sniffled loudly. Startled by her friend's now confident tone, Erica listened intently. "Hey, whatever happened is done. Maybe if we read her diary it will help us find out what's wrong, what's making her...what's making her want to lose so much weight—"

"*And* lose her best friends?" Erica added what to her made sense. She countered with her own proposal hoping to sound equally confident: "No. I think we have to call her and give it back."

"Not before we read it!" Jeanna sprang from the bed and stood before Erica. "Are you crazy? We can find out so much from that book! We'll be able to help her...Besides," Jeanna added coldly, "Even if we don't read it, she'll never believe we didn't so we might as well read it."

Erica strained to ignore the logical argument. "It's not right, Jeanna…You've never kept a diary." Erica brushed past Jeanna and sat on the edge of her bed shaking her head. "You don't know how private they are."

"Yeah? Well I do know that teachers are always saying that writing helps you get things out!" Rushing to the bed, Jeanna knelt behind Erica. She leaned back on her heels, grabbed a pillow and punched it. "And I bet," she said emphatically, "that anyone who keeps a diary in the first place is writing things they can't get out any other way." She threw the pillow aside punctuating her last statement.

Jeanna's words stung the back of Erica's head like needles. Her glazed eyes stared at her sneakers. She struggled to find the strength (not strength) to ignore the unintentional (perhaps) accusation. Erica drew in a large breath, turned to face Jeanna and exhaled: "It's not right."

Jeanna got up from the bed and grabbed her bag. "Fine." She unzipped the bag sharply and when she found the book flung it onto the bed. "But *you* can give it back to her!" she shouted. "Tell her *you* found the thief who took it. I'm leaving."

"Wait!" Erica rushed to block her friend's path. "I've already lost one best friend. I won't lose you, too." The girls searched each other's eyes. Waiting. Apologizing. Erica finally spoke. "Oh, I wish my mother was home!" She touched Jeanna's hand and surrendered. "Okay. We'll do this your way."

Erica walked to her bed and picked up the book. She joined Jeanna who had seated herself cross-legged on the floor at the foot of the bed. Erica opened the diary. The girls looked at each other solemnly then, beginning with August ninth, read in silence messages that randomly revealed themselves.

※※※※※※※

August 9

Dear Shiloh,

Maybe I've been wrong about Sandy. I still hate her for stealing Daddy away from Mom but she isn't all that bad. She took me to the mall today. The mall here makes ours look pathetic. It's awesome. She told me to buy anything I wanted to. Of course I knew Daddy would be footing the bill, but when did Mom ever say that? Daddy probably told Mom to let me get anything I wanted to, but did she ever let me? No. It was always "Money doesn't grow on trees" or "Buy something practical."

I got two pairs of Donna Karan jeans and a Louis V backpack. If you hear a loud roar some time soon, it'll be Daddy when he sees the bill.

Not missing Dulls-ville,
Kimberly

August 16

Dear Shiloh,

Dad prepared dinner again today. Can you believe it? Me neither. I mean all the time he lived home with me and Mom, I never once saw him make dinner. Mom knocked herself out making him fabulous gourmet meals and she always had to fish for compliments. "How is it honey?" or "This is a new recipe, do you like it?" Sick. He'd say yeah, good, or nod while he kept stuffing his face. I'd sooner die than humiliate myself like Mom did.

Anyway, he prepares this enormous seafood salad, sits it in a huge bread bowl that he hollowed out himself, serves us all at the table—that he set himself by the way—and Sandy doesn't touch it! I mean she almost literally doesn't touch it. Me, I could have devoured the whole thing by myself—it was just like Mom's only with a much lighter dressing. Does he say anything to her? Does he ask her how come she's not eating or say, "Honey, don't you like it?" No way. He watches her play with her food and says, "You've hardly touched your food, baby. Is that how you stay so beautiful?" Ugh. Can you believe it?

> Bored to death,
> Kimberly

P.S. Do you think Dad left Mom because of her weight?

August 21

Dearest Shiloh,

I can't wait for summer to be over. I miss Mom, I'm tired shopping and I hate these two lovebirds. Doesn't Daddy know I have feelings too? Today he came home from work complaining he was tired. Before I could even say anything—and I would have said something nice—Sandy as usual was all over him—poor baby, poor darling. She tells him to get into his bathing suit and go straight to the lounge chair where she will—in her words—relieve his stress. What am I, invisible? He walks like a robot into his room, comes out with his swimsuit on, plops in his damn lounge chair and I swear, stayed there practically forever letting her massage his head, his back and lord knows what else. Ugh. It was seven o'clock before they even remembered me. By then I was watching TV, I can assure you, acting like I didn't even notice the time.

I'm just in their way. Why did he take me for the whole summer again if she's here permanently now? I didn't ask to be here. I didn't ask him to leave Mom and find some skinny goddess to make him happy. This is the last year I give up my whole summer so he can ease his conscience.

I'm pretty hungry right now because the two love birds decided to go out and asked me to make something for myself unless I wanted them to bring me something. As if! I told them I wasn't hungry so it didn't matter—not that they cared. Thin is in around here or haven't I told you? Maybe I can get as thin and gorgeous as Sandy? Fat chance, huh? And I do mean FAT!

                    Counting the days till I'm home,
                    Kim

                    August 22

Shiloh,

I don't know if I can tell you how I'm feeling or what I'm feeling right now. We were at Sandy's parents house today for her father's birthday party. When it came time for cake, I went over to get a piece and do you know what Daddy said and I don't care if he was kidding. He said he was kidding but I don't care. Daddy said, "Don't take a big piece, honey. You don't want to end up like your mother, do you?" I ran from him and now he's pissed because he says I embarrassed him in front of Sandy's family. DO I CARE?

I feel so fat. A tiny part of me knows I'm not, but near Sandy I feel like a walrus. I probably look like one to Daddy.

How could he talk about Mommy that way? He keeps saying I took it the wrong way and Mom is wonderful and I have so many of her wonderful qualities. What? That I'm pleasantly plump. That I never speak up for myself? That I let him say and do anything he wants without making him admit he's the one that's wrong maybe once in a while? That I pretend everything's okay hoping that maybe one day it will be? Oh, who cares? I don't. It's too late.

Kimberly

September 1

Hey Shiloh,

Sanctuary! Sanctuary! I feel like singing, screaming—both. On our way home we had to stop at the Shady Lodge Adult Home to visit Sandy's grandmother—she probably plans to stay on the old lady's good side in case she leaves an inheritance. Anyway, I met the neatest lady while I was there. They made me hang out in a kind of recreation area for the residents. I felt sorry for them but they seemed to be satisfied enough playing cards or singing to the music this really neat old lady was playing on a piano. You'll never guess what her name is. Mars. Not the candy bar. The planet! Can you imagine? When she spotted me listening to her music she smiled at me and winked. I went over to her and told her how great she played. She asked me my name and she told me hers: "Mars…Mars Perri's my name," she said. The look on my face when I heard her name must have amused her because she told me how she got it. It's the neatest story.

ANNE HANSON

She said she was named after her mother's best friend, Mars, who had a twin sister whose name was, get ready, Venus. Really! She told me that when her friend's father had gotten word that his wife had given birth to twin girls, he ran all the way home from work. When he looked up and noticed the two planets shining, he took it as a sign and named his new daughters, Venus and Mars. I laughed when Mars told me she's always been grateful her mother's best friend hadn't been the other twin, Venus. What a scream!

Mars is sharp for an old lady. She said I looked unhappy. She asked me why and you know what? I told her. I told her everything I tell you. She cared. She really cared. She made me feel better just by listening. I told her about Mom and Dad and Sandy and how I hate my whole life. I told her how I hate them all for shuttling me around at their convenience. She asked me if I'd told them as much and when I said of course not, she asked so innocently, why not? It made me wonder—why hadn't I? I tried to explain to Mars that Mom and Dad weren't exactly The Brady Bunch kind of parents. She laughed. I laughed too. Mars understood completely. She told me all about herself. She said her father stopped loving her after her mother had died at childbirth. She said she always felt like a Cinderella, cooking and cleaning for her younger brother, an infant sister, and her father. I told her I would have run away. And I would have!

The whole time we talked she played her piano. She told me she was once a piano teacher and that she studied all her life. She said she practiced three, four, sometimes five hours a day. Can you imagine? She said in order to be very good at anything you had to practice till it hurt. Something, huh? I hope I get to talk with her again. She told me I could call her anytime. She sure made me feel good. I told her I hated myself. That really got us talking. And somehow it helped. I almost felt—normal. I haven't felt that way in a long time. I hope I made her feel good, too.

> Glad to be home,
> Kim

September 4

Dear Shiloh,

I still haven't returned Erica and Jeanna's calls. Just not ready for anyone yet. I ran into Amy and Jenell, though—they had lousy summers, too. We started talking about our messed up parents and then somehow got to talking about how we hate ourselves. It's nice to know someone else feels as miserable as I do. We got to talking about diets after Jenell complained she gained five pounds this summer at her dad's. We came up with this neat plan. You know how I always gain weight around holiday time and how all my New Year's resolutions are about losing what I gained? Well, this year forget about that. Amy, me, and Jenell have decided to lose enough weight now, so even when we oink out over the holidays, it won't be a big deal. Isn't that great! I didn't tell them but I kind of believe if I can lose that much weight, why would I want to blow it by gaining it back? It won't be hard to lose weight. With all the meals I've skipped this summer at Dad's Fat Farm, I'm a pro. By the way, I actually lost four pounds while I was there so how bad was it, really? Still, I do have a long way to go to look half way decent.

I wish one of Mom's diets would work for her. She sure tries them all. Maybe I could help—No, never mind. I know she'd throw a fit if she thought I was trying to lose weight. All I've heard since I came home is how thin she thinks I am. Not to be mean or anything, but next to her...you know.

> Energetically yours,
> Kimberly

✳✳✳✳✳✳✳

Erica closed the book. She had read enough. Kim's secrets throbbed in her head. More puzzle pieces. She realized for the first time that Kim's situation was far too complex for well-intentioned friends. The diary's passages extinguished her every naive hope. She had no idea how to help her friend.

She barely heard the phone ring. She turned to Jeanna who looked equally overwhelmed. "That's probably Kim looking for her book." For an instant Erica needed to hug Jeanna, but she knew no hug would quell her fear. She suspected Jeanna felt the same. "Please go, Jeanna. I'd better talk to her alone."

The girls helped each other up from the floor and before Jeanna walked to the door, Jeanna asked hesitantly, "Friends?"

"Friends," Erica replied sincerely as she lifted the phone to her ear. "Hello?"

She heard silence. Then a click.

X
Confrontation

Kim slammed the phone into its cradle. She paced her room, fell onto her knees searching, scouring one more time, every inch of carpet under her bed. She pounded her fist and jumped up. No. The phone was too easy. Confronting the thieves face to face would be much more satisfying. Wearing her baggy jeans and oversized plaid flannel shirt, she hurriedly put on her socks and sneakers, strangling knots into her shoelaces. She bolted from the bedroom, slamming her door.

"Where are you going?" Mrs. Spencer called from the kitchen.

"Out!" Kim barked.

"Get over here now," Mrs. Spencer yelled.

Kim stormed into the kitchen. "What?"

"Watch that tone for one thing…and sit down for another." Mrs. Spencer waited for Kim to cooperate. "You watch how you speak to me, young lady, and when you are about to leave this house…if I ask you where you are going…I expect more than 'Out'…Do you understand?" Mrs. Spencer immediately regretted her unexpected show of strength. She put down a half-peeled potato and wiped her moist hands on her apron. She sat down at the kitchen table while Kim remained standing, staring at her forefinger tracing the table's edge.

Mrs. Spencer wanted to apologize. Wanted to ask the questions that raced through her mind ever since Kim had come home this summer. Kim always acted distant whenever she returned from long or short visits with her father. But after this extended summer visit, she had come back more distant, different. She was pale. And quiet. And she hardly ate. Was she depressed? Had something happened? Always afraid Kim would rather be living with her father who could give her everything, Mrs. Spencer had purposefully avoided asking questions that might upset her daughter—or yield answers she did not want to hear. Hesitantly she now risked: "Kim, What's wrong? Are you okay?"

"I'm fine," Kim said flatly. She refused to look at her mother who struggled to continue.

"Did you have a fight with Jeanna?"

"Mom, I don't want to talk about it now, all right?" Kim finally looked up and her scowl persuaded her mother to change the subject—and to ignore the fact that Kim had (defiantly?) remained standing.

"I'll be on the graveyard shift tonight. I'm covering in maternity."

"I thought you were off today?" Kim welcomed this safe territory. While Mrs. Spencer explained she was covering for a friend, Kim thought about how much she loved her mother. More than her mother knew. More than she would ever tell her. Kim had always felt angry that her mother had not somehow prevented the divorce. She didn't understand why she blamed her mother more than her father. She just knew that she did.

Kim sat down but heard little of the taking-the-extra-work-for-extra-money explanation. She heard, instead, voices. Past voices. Her mother's cries when her father had asked for the divorce. His icy words. Her futile pleas. A panorama of unwelcomed scenes replayed in her mind and Kim vowed (once again) she would never let a man see her care as much as her mother had. Mom's a good person, and if Dad doesn't know it, that's his problem not hers.

So what if Mom isn't gorgeous? Kim could almost hear her mother complaining: *Well, I've gone from okay* (goal weight) *to not-okay* (weight gain) or sometimes, like now, *to very not-okay* (bigger weight gain).

Listening to her private thoughts and not her mother's babble, Kim's assessment of her mother was unshaken: a good person though a bit dysfunctional. She inwardly smiled. She longed to tell her mother that although she hated the divorce, she understood it, too, though she didn't know how such conflicting feelings were possible. She longed to rush to her mother, hug her, tell her everything would be okay. Instead she said, "I have to go to Erica's for a while, Mom. I promise I won't be gone long."

"Well, I still think it's too close to dinner to be going out." By now Mrs. Spencer was standing and rather than hold her daughter closely (which in fact she ached to do) she chided, "Be back before seven because that's when we'll be eating."

"No problem." Kim gave her mother a quick but sincere kiss on her cheek and forced an airy good-bye as she shut the door.

Mrs. Spencer returned to the counter and grabbed the half-peeled potato. "And tonight I'll make sure you eat."

XI
Retaliation

"Where's my book, Erica?" Kim stood at Erica's front door, arms folded, right foot rapidly tapping the door mat.

"I'm so sorry, Kim! Jeanna never meant to take it. She just...we thought—"

"I don't want to hear it, Erica. Just give me my diary!" she yelled. "I called Jeanna first and got no answer so I knew where to call next. And I don't care what Jeanna meant and I don't care what you think—"

"You don't have to tell me that!" Erica tried to match Kim's tone and posture. "That was rather obvious when you threw my letter out. And I'm not doing or saying another thing until you come inside my house. Shouting in front of my house like this is ridiculous."

Without comment Kim brushed roughly past Erica and stormed up the stairs to Erica's bedroom. Erica followed helplessly and closed her bedroom door. "Give me the book," Kim said. The voice was soft, the tone flat, the effect chilling.

Erica strained against the ache in her throat and swallowed hard. Please don't cry. Be mad. Don't let her see that you care. She stepped over to her desk to get the book. Stay mad. Her plan almost worked until the picture above her desk caught her eye; there was chubby Cynthia offering sweets to her dear bunny friends. Tears conquered her resolve and the picture blurred. She blinked hard and breathed deeply and the picture became clear again. "Kim." Erica turned offering her friend the diary. "Jeanna was wrong. We were wrong. I know that, and she knows that. When you threw my letter away, I knew you didn't want to hear my advice. So I sent Jeanna over to—"

"Steal my diary!"

"No!" Erica begged. "To sit with you, talk with you, try to understand what's going on. You've been so different lately." Erica approached her with the diary.

Kim unfolded her arms only long enough to grab the book; she immediately resumed her hostile position, her right hand now shielding the book under her left arm. "You're nuts. The two of you...nuts." Now that she had the book, her tone was almost light. "I go on a little diet and you two go nuts. What's with you?!"

Erica hoped that Kim's tight smile was a conciliatory gesture and prayed for the right words. She moved toward her bed and sat down, wordlessly inviting Kim to do the same. Kim sat on the wicker rocker by the window instead, and Erica nodded her gratitude. "I'm sorry, Kim," she began. "I'm sorry about all of this and I'm sorry if sending you that letter upset you..."I know dieting is no big deal...everybody diets." Erica suddenly needed to inhale deeply and quickly and did so before adding, "I know everyone could afford to lose a few pounds..." Erica chose to ignore the sneering accusation in Kim's expression and

THIN VEILS

continued with strained nonchalance. "How tall are you, Kim?"

"Five-three," Kim snapped suspiciously. "Why?"

"I was just wondering. How much weight would you have to lose to get down to eighty-five pounds?" When Kim leaned forward in the chair, Erica panicked and gushed, "It's just that I might want to join you and Amy and Jenell if you'll let me. Hell," she said as airily as possible, "if anyone has to lose weight around here, it's me."

Shaking her head slowly, Kim sucked in her cheeks and bit down until they hurt too much. She pursed her lips then tisked loudly. "Drop it, Erica. Just drop it…" She rose from the creaking rocker, "because it's not going to work."

"Kim, wait! You're my friend. I love you!" Surprised and encouraged when Kim sat back down, Erica spoke softly: "Think. You're five-three. You've obviously lost weight since you came back from your dad's. And you've lost more since school started. You're not fooling me behind baggy clothes, so what's the deal?" Erica realized her apologetic tone was now indicting, but she risked it: "Bulimia or anorexia?"

Kim stormed over to Erica who stood to face her. "How dare you! What's the matter? Are you jealous? I lose a little weight so you think I'm sick? Well, sorry to disappoint you, Erica, but I'm on a diet. Just a diet, get it? Now get out of my life and leave me alone!"

As Kim stormed toward the door mumbling, "I can't belive this crap," Erica blurted out: "I read some of your diary, Kim."

Kim was halfway down the stairs before she turned to Erica, who stood helplessly by her doorway. "Oh, I

63

had no doubt about that, Erica...I hope you and Jeanna enjoyed yourselves."

Enraged, Kim gasped for each breath, pounding down the remaining steps, resisting the urge to scream. Philip met her at the bottom of the staircase. "Hi, Kim," he said brightly, but Kim did not hear or see him. He watched her leave.

XII
Is Anybody Listening?

Erica spotted Richie and Steve laughing and pushing each other good-naturedly. She caught up to them and asked, "Hey, guys. What's so funny? I can use a laugh."

As they continued their walk to the cafeteria, Richie explained. "You had to be there. Jimmy King was doing his usual routine in Carlson's class and she finally gave him detention. When the bell rings she calls him to her desk and hands the pink slip to him—he must've forgot he was getting it 'cause he yells, 'Where do you get off giving me a detention!?'"

Steve took over. "Well everybody that's still in the classroom hears him and Carlson goes ballistic. She tears her desk drawer open, flings out a referral, and when she looks up—man, was her face red—Jimmy's gone! I mean he just flat out walked away from her. She races to the door after him—me and Richie are just hanging out for the show—she's writing out the referral all the while she's storming after him. She stops by the door and that's when we spot the principal—"

"Yeah fine, Steve." Richie repossessed his story. "Let me finish. We pass by Carlson...she still has her head down like she's writing the Constitution—she doesn't even see Mr. Walker standing there when he says, 'Hello, Mrs. Carlson. Do you mind if I sit in on your class this hour?'" Richie choked with laughter after imitating the principal's deep voice and once again lost his story to Steve.

"You had to see the look on her face...oh man, it was so funny...'Huh, wha, ah, oh, of course, Mr. Walker,'" Steve mimicked in a high-pitched falsetto. "I don't know what she said after that. I was ready to laugh right in front of her so I grabbed Richie and took off. She's gonna slaughter Jimmy tomorrow. James King is gonna be history."

Richie quipped, "You mean *King* James." (On the second day of school in front of her entire fourth hour English class, Mrs. Carlson had sarcastically reprimanded Jimmy, explaining to him that King was his surname and not his title. Her cutting humor had since caused her quite a bit of embarrassment as students teasingly reminded her Jimmy had the royal right to misbehave.)

The story was a welcome relief. Last night Erica had been alone with Philip. Her mother was at a Parents Without Partners meeting that Marilyn Grayson had recommended she attend, and Erica wouldn't speak to anyone else about her confrontation with Kim, not even Jeanna.

Erica inched her way through the painfully slow lunch line, half listening to her two friends whose voices competed with several others: *Tiffany loves the new guy, Peter...Tom overheard Greg threatening to fight what's his name...How come the fried chicken nuggets look like rocks?* At this, Erica smiled wistfully; at least part of her life was still normal enough to recognize and appreciate humor.

She followed Steve and Richie to their usual table. She maneuvered them so that they, not she, were facing the south wall table where, predictably, Kim, Amy and Jenell were seated. "Guys, can you see if there's any food at Kim's table?" Steve, having the best view, raised his head a bit then lowered it without breaking his chewing rhythm. He swallowed the huge bite of his meatball hero. "Nope. Just pop cans."

"Pop cans?" Erica fought the impulse to turn around. "They can't drink pop at lunch. It's against—"

"Yeah well, they ain't anymore. Some aide is making Jenell throw the cans out."

"Could you tell if they were diet or not?"

"What do you think I've got, eagle eyes?" Steve snapped. "Besides, who cares?"

All the while, Richie silently ate his chicken, studying each piece as if to determine them sedimentary or metamorphic.

"Richie, what do you think…about Kim, I mean?" Erica asked timidly.

Richie had hoped to remain silent, to keep his feelings about Kim private. Unable to hide his frustration with the situation—and with Erica—any longer he snapped, "No, Erica, what do *you* think?…She used to sit with us last year. All of us…and Jeanna, too, when she had the same lunch hour. Now where is she?" He made it sound like a simple arithmetic problem.

"So, I guess you two have really broken up for good. Did you talk to her at all before you broke up? Did you tell her that you were worried about her? Did you—"

"Look, Erica, we've been over this a million times." Using his buttered roll as a finger, Richie pointed. "When Kim came back this summer, I told her she looked great. I was glad to see her. She said it was because she lost weight. That's not why I said it. I hardly noticed. I said it because I *was* glad to see her. I let it slide. No big deal. Then when I heard her idiot friends were doing this stupid diet thing, I talked to her...or at least I tried to talk to her. When that didn't work I wrote her a letter. I told her she was acting stupid." Richie's matter-of-fact tone never altered. "But there was no getting through to her, so I dropped it...and her. She wants to act like a jerk, let her. You should drop it, too, Erica."

"We can't just drop it!" Erica pleaded.

Richie's roll now hung, mid-bite, between his teeth.

"She's our friend! She can't afford to lose another ounce! She's going to get sick if she tries to lose more weight."

Richie stared a moment longer at Erica and then bit down hard. "Erica," he mumbled, "eat your chicken."

"I don't know why anybody would try to lose weight," Steve said, jabbing his plastic fork at the bits of meatball that had fallen from his sandwich, "unless they really had to...I mean if they were fat or wanted to make a team or something." More loudly he added, "And I don't know how they expect you to eat around here when they give you a plastic spoon that's trying to be a fork!"

Erica's frustration rose with an audible sigh. Almost reacting to Steve's glib indifference, she reacted instead to a question that had emerged: Was

Steve still dieting to make the wrestling team? How do I ask tactfully without insulting him, she thought. The last thing Erica wanted to do was alienate another friend.

"I agree, Steve. I mean, unless people were obese…"

"Fat," Richie said flatly. A year older than most his friends having been retained years before, Richie occasionally pulled rank.

"Obese," Erica insisted. "Too many people, who have no real reason to lose weight, try to lose it anyway. They are just falling into society's trap.

"Yes, Doctor Shepherd," Richie said bowing irreverently.

Time passed and amidst bites, chews and swallows, Erica retreated from their prattle to gather arguments from her night of fierce reflection. "Will you guys please listen? I know what I'm saying. Do you remember that health unit last year…about body image? Mrs. Duffy rattled on about how we've all been brainwashed to think that if we buy certain stuff or eat certain stuff we will have perfect love lives, perfect skin, perfect bodies?"

Erica nudged her chair closer to the table and whispered excitedly. "Well, she was right. We don't do anything or buy anything for ourselves…unless it's something we think will help us get that perfect boyfriend or girlfriend or perfect complexion or perfect body—only it's not even our own idea of perfect!

"Take me. I'm not obese but I try to lose weight sometimes, and those times are when I let society dictate to me that the way I look is not okay." In the silence that followed Erica hoped it had been safe to reveal so much of herself. Her fragile hope was crushed by Steve.

"Erica, what does any of that have to do with Kim's diet?" After licking sauce from his pinkie, he added, "Quit preaching and let us eat in peace. Besides...not everyone cares. I mean...look at you, Erica. You said it yourself. You could lose some weight. What are you, about one thirty, one thirty-five? But you don't care, and we don't either. Who cares about that perfect image crap? I mean...we still love you."

Erica swallowed hard, not hearing the last. Her stomach burned. She held a napkin to her lips wondering how she had set herself up like this. How could Steve be so cruel? And wrong. Not wrong. Not completely. She did care. But a haughty attitude was so much easier to maintain than a weight loss. Hurt turned to angry resolve and she retaliated: "Well how about you, Steve? Are you trying to lose weight for yourself or for your coach?"

"Give it a break, Erica," Steve whined. "It's not the same thing. My coach sure ain't my boyfriend."

"Of course not." She found her hook. "But don't you see? You were content with yourself until Coach Hawks threatened to cut you off the team."

"Yeah. Well," Steve said dejectedly, "I'm off the team...indefinitely...but I'm still here, and I'm not on a whacko diet. Hell, I tried, but man, dieting is a pain in the butt."

"Watch your mouth, young man," an aide within earshot called out perfunctorily. Steve nodded in kind, while Erica ignored the interruption.

"Well, I think you're stronger than most people in this cafeteria, Steve, because you made your own decision."

"Well, thank you very much, doctor," Steve teased.

Erica forced her feelings down with her last nugget to capitalize on Steve's lightened mood. Here was an opportunity to support her theory. "But, Steve, think about it. What happens to someone...someone emotionally wired...from a divorce, let's say...and she hates her father, her mother, her whole life. Couldn't she go over the edge, lose her own self-image...buy into the packaged dream of perfection hoping that it's true, hoping...until it becomes a nightmare?"

The aide tapped their table with her whistle and Richie, relieved by the early cleanup signal, stacked their littered trays and got up. "I'm outta here."

Steve's frustrated stare prompted Erica to ask a different question: "Are you upset about not making the team?"

"Sometimes..." More softly than he had yet spoken, Steve continued. "Sometimes I think I'll miss it. I mean six pounds isn't so much to lose. But when I was trying to lose it, I was making myself crazy. I couldn't lose an ounce and I was practically starving myself! Then I'd get so hungry, I'd drink a quart of milk and eat a loaf of bread smeared with butter! My dad got me a plastic sweat suit to run in. He even biked alongside me...." When Richie returned, Steve hesitated; his glazed eyes searched Richie's for a moment and he decided to continue. "I lost two pounds after every run but by the next morning they were back. I was fighting with my sister worse than usual and everyone got fed up with me. Everybody, even my dad, said to quit. So I did…Sometimes I think of trying again. I still have time."

Erica hit the table with her palm. "No—Ow!" She rubbed the sting. "Don't do it! I remember reading an article about coaches who got in trouble for forcing their athletes to stay under weight to meet division weights…You can ruin your health," Erica wailed.

"Yes, Mommy," Steve teased. Richie groaned, "Oh, give it a rest, Erica."

"Yeah, well…" Steve leaned back stretching his arms above his head. "All those neat ribbons and medals that I *won't* get this year because I can't lose a few lousy pounds…I don't know…" He lowered his arms and folded them across his broad chest. "I'm not sure sometimes if I am doing the right thing. My dad says he'll help me if I want to try again—as long as I promise not to drive everyone crazy."

As the bell rang, Erica heaved a sigh: Oh that's just great.

XIII
Unwelcomed News

In the two weeks that followed the diary incident, except for the inescapable first and last hour classes, Kim had avoided Erica completely. And with memory of their last confrontation painfully clear Erica welcomed the distance. Kim had severed ties with all her friends even Richie. Though Richie insisted that he had broken up with Kim, he was unable to suppress the prevailing between-class rumor initiated by Jenell: Kim had dumped him, sick of his private pleas for her to "eat something" and the prospect of hanging with a guy who acted more like a parent than a boyfriend. The last thing Kim needed was another parent. The fact that he and not Kim had drawn the sympathy of friends only made him feel worse.

Schoolwork and the demands of the Harvest Dance, now just weeks away, filled Erica's days. There were flyers to design, decorations to consider, DJs to interview. There was no time for Kim, who during this time had begun wearing wire-rimmed sunglasses and two oversized flannel shirts of contrasting colors and pattern, outer shirt unbuttoned, sleeves rolled high. Erica had dismissed the unusual style as another Kim Spencer fashion statement, until today, when she saw through the deception to Kim's dramatic weight loss.

Arriving home from school Erica opened her front door to see Philip petting Diamond's creamy white stomach. The cat's blue eyes sparkled as he leaned toward Erica inviting her to partake in the occasional welcome ritual. As if sensing Erica's somber mood, Diamond twisted himself upright and scampered away. "Guess he had enough," Erica said flatly.

"Guess so," Philip chimed.

Erica tossed her bag on top of the wicker trunk that stood in the hall and plodded into the kitchen. "Hi, Mom, you're home early."

"Well, I'm not really early," she mumbled. "It's just that I'm home on time for a change."

"Yeah, really," Erica quipped.

Gail looked up from her magazine. "When you're working, and time-and-a-half becomes a relevant term, you'll understand."

Erica smiled at her mother's good-natured tease. "Whatya' reading?"

"A good story," she murmured as she hurriedly flicked through pages to find page forty-eight.

"Can it wait?" Erica asked apologetically.

Though Gail did not want to look up, she did. She saw her daughter's worried look for the first time. "Yes, it can wait," she said deliberately. "What's wrong?"

"I need to talk with you."

Gail left her seat and joined Erica in the den area. They sat facing each other in matching rattan chairs. The rattan creaked as Erica forced each of her sneakers off with her heels. She tucked her feet under her, wriggled herself into the round cushion until she was comfortable. She hugged a pillow to her chest.

Gail listened to her daughter and interrupted thoughtfully. Yes, Erica should be worried. No, it didn't matter why it took Erica so long to tell her about the diary and yes, Jeanna was wrong to take it. No, they should not have read the passages and yes, she understood why they had read them. Gail had snuggled into a position similar to her daughter's. She felt relieved and almost proud that Erica had confided in her about the diary, her helplessness, her guilt. She too felt guilt; her daughter had held so much in for so long and she hadn't noticed. Did Erica settle for me? Would she have confided in her father sooner if he were still here for her? She quickly disconnected from her negative path and said, "Erica, I think you're right. Kim does have a serious problem. She may be anorexic. Part of me wants to call her mother, but the other part of me knows Linda still isn't dealing with her divorce. I'd just be heaping on more pain telling her what we know…But she can't be oblivious to all this, can she?" Gail lifted herself awkwardly from the plush cushion. Speaking more to herself than to Erica, she declared: "She's a nurse, for heaven's sakes! She's got to see beyond baggy shirts and pants, doesn't she?!"

As if in reply the phone rang, startling both mother and daughter. "Linda, hello!" Gail's eyes widened and she repeatedly pointed into the receiver, emphasizing to Erica the irony of who had called.

"No, that's okay. Don't be silly…Is she?" Gail's tone changed. "Oh, I'm so sorry…Yes, of course. I would be, too, Linda."

Erica sat upright, frustrated by hearing half the conversation. "Yes. To tell you honestly, Erica was just telling me she noticed. She's been very concerned about Kim." Erica was out of her chair. Still hugging the pillow, she marched out of the den, back into it, and out again. She remained in the den when she angrily realized her useless pacing prevented her from hearing at least her mother's half of the conversation.

"...I can imagine. I wouldn't know what to do either." Erica's eyes followed her mother whose own eyes seemed to study her feet as they dragged several steps forward then back. Gail's short golden brown hair had pitched straight down covering her face almost completely. "Yes, that's a good idea…Oh, yes, at least for one day. And stop blaming yourself. You can't shove food down her throat."

Dropping the pillow, Erica threw her hands to her head and rubbed her scalp hard. She raked her fingers through her thick black hair as if the gesture would clear her mother's hidden expression. What was Mrs. Spencer telling her?

The instant her mother hung up, Erica cried, "What's happened, Mom?"

"Kim fainted at school today."

"That's impossible!" Erica protested. "I would have heard. It would have been all over school."

Gail took Erica by the hand and guided her to a kitchen chair. "It happened in the nurse's office. Apparently Kim went there because she was feeling lightheaded. Linda got a call at work to pick up her daughter. That's when the nurse told her about Kim's diet.

"How did the nurse find out?" Erica rose slightly from her chair but Gail's gentle touch restrained her. She sat beside her daughter.

"Believe it or not, Kim told the nurse everything. Fainting obviously scared her, thank goodness. Linda said when she got Kim home and helped her into bed, Kim felt like skin and bones. She's running a slight fever now."

Erica folded her arms on the table and lay her head down wearily. "Oh, God. I can't believe this. I should have seen this coming," she sobbed. She looked up at her mother desperately. "I only noticed today how skinny she got. I was so angry at her for being mad at me, I ignored her every chance I got. She wasn't in English this afternoon but I just figured she'd cut class again. She's been doing that a lot…It's all my fault. I should have done something."

"Erica, stop blaming yourself…it's not going to help." As she spoke, Gail gently rubbed her daughter's back. "Linda told me the school nurse gave her the phone numbers of several counselors who specialize in eating disorders. Marilyn's name is on the list and I recommended her. She said she'd think about calling but…" Gail stopped rubbing Erica's back, rose from her chair abruptly and, sighing, added, "but she wants to call Kim's father first to get *his* advice."

Fueled by Mrs. Spencer's hesitancy Gail was filled with as much frustration as Erica. She poured cold water from the refrigerator's dispenser thinking, I can't believe after all this time she still relies on him. Doesn't she know the first thing about doing anything for herself? Staring into her glass, she drank the water slowly, privately disturbed. Did she envy Linda's ability to contact her husband even though he was gone? She put the glass down and picked up the phone.

"Who are you calling, Mom?" Erica whimpered.

"I'm calling Marilyn Grayson," Gail snapped. "She gets paid to deal with this stuff!"

Erica watched her mother with expectancy and became bewildered when she heard her mother sneer, "Yeah, yeah, yeah," but understood when she recited: "Yes, hi, Marilyn. This is Gail Shepherd. Give me a call when you get in. It's important. It's for your *professional* advice."

Fighting the sadness that weighed her down, Erica got up slowly from her chair. She didn't notice her mother who looked on helplessly. She walked through the hall, up the stairs and into her room. She barely heard Philip shout he was hungry. She did not bother to close her bedroom door. Collapsing on her bed, she rolled onto her back, clasped her hands under her head and stared at her ceiling.

Erica felt a tear slide into her hair. She sniffled and grew angry that congestion might invade her privacy and force her to get up for a tissue. Sniffling more forcefully she turned and saw the picture on her wall. There were her bunnies. Bittersweet memories flooded her mind. Innocent games of pretend with her best friends. Innocence annihilated by some strange and scary force she didn't understand at all. Erica sprang from her bed to the bathroom, suffocated and blinded by tears she could control no longer.

She splashed cool water on her face and welcomed its immediate though temporary relief. She looked in the mirror studying the fullness of her cheeks and the blemish (never pimple!) that was threatening to emerge. Ugly, a voice within her snickered. She recalled Steve's thoughtless words and buried her face in a towel. Why couldn't I be built like my mother she asked the plush terry cloth. An image of Gail's thin frame appeared, gray jogging suit hanging loosely about her. Erica dropped the towel and once again faced the mirror. *My poor mother. I'm upset, I've got her upset, and all I can do is envy her body. Like she needs any of this. Oh, I wish it would go away. All of it!* Just as Erica was about to hide her face with her hands, she stopped. Instead, she dropped her hands to her side, squinted at her reflection for a long moment, then sniffled her way out of the depressing reverie: "I am pretty and I am me!" she declared too loudly. She stared one more moment then decided she had won this round with the voice that periodically challenged her self-esteem.

The relief of the cool water lingered this time. Erica dried her face and headed straight for her phone. "Jeanna, stop whatever you're doing and come over right now."

"I can't. My—"

"Don't tell me you can't!" Erica shouted. "This is majorly important."

"Well, I'll be majorly in trouble if I leave before my parents come home," Jeanna retaliated.

"Leave them a note!" Erica insisted.

Jeanna was unfazed. "Last time I left a note, they gave me their lecture on what-if-this-that-and-the-other-thing-had-happened-while-you-were-gone? I was grounded for a week, and I don't need that again, thank you. What's the matter, anyway? Is it Kim?"

"Yes, it's Kim. She passed out at school today, that's what's the matter."

"I'll be right over." Jeanna hung up her phone. As she scrawled a note, Jeanna thought, "My parents are gonna kill me this time."

✺✺✺✺✺✺✺

It was Philip who answered the door when Jeanna rang the bell. Standing erect and peering seriously into her eyes, he declared, "Erica said for me to say: 'Tell Jeanna to come right upstairs as soon as she gets here.'" Amused by Philip's faulty attempt at accuracy, Jeanna leaned over and kissed his forehead before running up the stairs. Philip added, "Are you eating with us? My mom said you can. We're having spaghetti." Jeanna didn't answer.

Erica rushed from her rocking chair when Jeanna entered her room and hugged her for a long time.

"Erica, tell me!" Jeanna was frightened. "Tell me what's happened." Jeanna sat attentively at the foot of the bed as Erica paced back and forth recounting all she knew.

"...And Mrs. Spencer's not doing anything until she talks to Kim's father. Can you believe it? Kim could be dying and her mother is not even doing anything!"

"Gosh, Erica, I don't get it. What do you expect her to do? What can she do?" Jeanna shifted to face Erica who had sat down beside her.

"She can at least call a counselor on the list she got. How can you ask such a question? At least calling a therapist to set up an appointment is a start. What if she can't get in touch with Kim's dad right away?

What if he's out of town on business? How long can Kim wait?"

"Kim's mother is a nurse," Jeanna reasoned. "She would know if Kim was in serious trouble."

Up Erica shot. "No, she wouldn't! She's in such denial it's pathetic. All she ever thinks about is herself and how miserable she is now! Why do you think it took something like this to get her to notice?"

Thoroughly confused by Erica's attack on Mrs. Spencer, Jeanna remained silent. Erica had always liked Kim's mother. Wasn't it Erica who rallied to Mrs. Spencer's side when Kim kept blaming her for the separation and divorce? Wasn't it Erica who sent a cheerful poem to Mrs. Spencer when the divorce was finalized. And didn't Erica once say she loved Mrs. Spencer and hoped to be a gourmet cook like her one day? The distant sound of a phone broke the silence. Erica rushed to her door, strained to hear her mother's voice, then left her room pounding down the stairs. Jeanna decided she simply would not budge until Erica returned, but less than a minute passed before she threw her hands up, dropped them to her sides, and rushed out of the bedroom to find Erica.

"That's my mom's friend on the phone!" Erica said excitedly, almost crashing into Jeanna who was on her way down the stairs as Erica was racing up.

"Who?" Jeanna groaned, angrily regretting she had risked big trouble with her parents for an evening of chaos with Erica Shepherd.

"You remember…the lady from my mom's building, the shrink! C'mon, help me set the table. Stay over. Mom said you can. I'll fill you in."

"You'd better."

While Erica and Jeanna set down placemats and dishes, Philip followed with forks and spoons. Understanding little of what his sister said, he listened halfheartedly while Jeanna listened fully.

"Grayson used to be real heavy, like one hundred pounds heavier than she is now, right, mom?"

"Right, Erica," Gail muttered as she stirred the sauce.

Erica spoke quickly, raising not dropping her voice at the end of each sentence. "She joined some—"

"Recovery group," her mother offered.

"Yeah...Now she's gorgeous. She became a therapist because she wanted to help people and she mainly does people with eating disorders because she knows she can help them best...right, Mom?"

"Well, I don't know exactly what you mean by 'does people with eating disorders...'" By now Gail was pouring spaghetti into a colander, while Philip, thoroughly bored by the conversation, stared at the cloud of steam. "But if you mean she *counsels* people with eating disorders, then right."

The table was set and the explanation complete as far as Erica was concerned, but Jeanna was not sure how all this information meant anything. "Can I call my house and see if my parents got home yet? I think this is gonna be a long night."

※※※※※※※

A horn honked and Jeanna hugged Erica. "'Gotta go. Bye!" Jeanna hurried to her father's car thinking that although the night was long, it had been successful for several reasons. First: She did not get in trouble with her parents who were equally concerned about Kim once Erica's mother had spoken to them about what had happened. Second: While feasting on a delicious spaghetti dinner in spite of the canned sauce (her mother always made it fresh) she learned why Erica had been so excited about Grayson's phone call. Months before, Marilyn Grayson had contacted local schools promoting her yearly workshop on self-esteem and eating disorders. Marilyn had regularly spoken at Erica's high school, but only to eleventh and twelfth grade students. *Until this year.* The principal had just phoned her about a "disquieting incident" at his school that made him realize it would perhaps be worthwhile to schedule her for all grade levels. (Jeanna and Erica had to promise Gail repeatedly they would say nothing at school about their advance knowledge.)

Jeanna turned, waved another good-bye to Erica, and smiled. There was one more reason the night had been successful: She was confident Kim would soon get the help she needed.

XIV

Betrayal

Kim was absent for two days. Each time Erica phoned, she listened to the same cheery voices asking the caller to leave a message and promising that Linda or Kim would return the call. Only neither of them ever did. Her mother's attempts were similarly futile. When Kim did not show up the third day, Erica resolved to get answers from Amy and Jenell during lunch hour. Snubbing them had not been very satisfying, and besides, surely they had kept contact with Kim.

As she approached their table Erica was surprised to see they were both eating the roast turkey special. She dropped her tray roughly and seized the opportunity. "What's this? Food? You're actually eating now that your stupid diet club got my best friend sick!" When Amy and Jenell looked down at their plates and said nothing, Erica dropped into a chair and struck her fist on the table. "What kind of friends are you, anyway? You knew she was losing too much weight. Why didn't you say anything? And how come you two look the same? You were on the same sick diet. How come you still look the same?" Erica slouched back and wondered: Why did they look the same? "I don't get it. Kim's really sick," she pleaded. "Amy, Jenell, one of you, say something! You can at least say something. And what are you looking at?" Erica barked at several girls at another table who had been watching and who, now, quickly turned away.

Amy raised her head slowly, while Jenell looked on quietly. "At first we thought it was a good idea, Erica. Everybody diets," Amy explained. "We figured if we did it together like a club we'd be helping each other."

"So you starved yourselves?...I'm sorry, I didn't mean that." She really did mean it, but Erica realized hostility might end the conversation abruptly.

Amy nodded and continued. "Erica, we didn't starve ourselves...that's just it..." Amy hesitated, looked at Jenell for support, then continued. "We couldn't do it. Kim kept insisting it was no big deal to skip meals...that she started doing it at her dad's and anyone could do it. But we couldn't do it. When Jenell and I got home from school we'd stuffed our faces with the nearest food we could get our hands on we were so hungry. We just didn't have the nerve to tell Kim. She was so determined. And it was easy for her!...We didn't know how to tell her we weren't really dieting...and she never seemed to notice."

Erica fought the urge to scream. For weeks they had hidden their deception and lied to her best friend. They had both stood by and watched Kim lose weight and health, yet said nothing. She whispered her assault. "Didn't you wonder why Kim hadn't noticed you weren't losing weight? Couldn't you tell it was a sign she didn't care about your stupid club any longer? That she had gone over the edge!"

"What could we have done?" Amy protested in a passionate whisper that matched Erica's. "You know Kim."

"When she started wearing those tinted John Lennon glasses," Jenell interrupted, "I knew it was to hide her dark circles." As if confessing she added, "but I said nothing. No...worse," Jenell cried, "I said I liked them."

Did Erica care to hear any more? No. She stood up, ready to assault them with language that would probably get her several lunch detentions when suddenly the loudspeaker blared: "Amy Peterson and Jenell Bismark, to guidance, please."

"It's probably about Kim again," Jenell muttered. Amy nodded. Together they rushed from their seats, and Erica, whose hostile posture deflated the moment they left.

She scanned the cafeteria for Steve and Richie and walked to their table when she spotted them. "Move over, guys," she said wearily. She plopped into the empty chair near Richie.

"What's the matter with you? Never mind. I know," Steve said apologetically. "Any news about Kim?"

Ignoring his question, Erica exclaimed, "Can you believe they let her become anorexic, when all the time they were eating behind her back?" If Richie or Steve replied, she did not hear them. Erica sat eating mechanically. She silently convinced herself to visit Kim's house after school. I'll force my way in if necessary. I have to know how Kim is. I have to help in anyway I can!

The lunch aide signaled their table's dismissal. As Steve got up he nodded at Erica and smiled, "Great company, huh, Rich?"

"Yeah. I hear she's trying out for Miss Pleasant at the Harvest Dance." Sensing that their well-intentioned tease had failed, they both shrugged and walked away.

The lunch aide tapped Erica. "Your table is clean. I said you can go now."

"No, I can't go now," Erica answered, still lost in her own thoughts: "I have to wait till school's over."

The aide furrowed her brow. "Huh?"

XV

Emptied Nest

Erica stood at Kim's front door while the what-ifs assaulted her, tempting her to run. What if her mother cries? What if Kim's too sick to see me? What if she's not even here? On and on until at last her stronger voice countered: Quit it, Erica. Just knock!

The door slowly opened. Mrs. Spencer nodded when she saw Erica. A weak smile signaled her to enter. The silence that followed them into the living room chilled Erica like a perilous fog. Mrs. Spencer sat down on the couch, busying her left hand's fingers on its floral pattern, clenching her right hand on her lap. Erica stood awkwardly until Mrs. Spencer finally noticed her and spoke. "Kim's not here. Her father took her."

"Took her?" Erica rushed to sit by Mrs. Spencer and embraced her.

Mrs. Spencer pulled back politely. "He said I didn't know how to take care of his daughter. *His* daughter. That she would be better off with him. That if she needed help, he'd get her the best help money could buy." Her eyes implored Erica to help her get control of her life that had been shattered—again—several days ago. The tired woman wanted someone to tell her everything was all right. She bit her lower lip to stop its quiver and stopped only when she felt the

THIN VEILS

pain. Tears pooled in her eyes and she began to weep into her hands.

Erica rubbed Mrs. Spencer's back gently. She felt embarrassed because here she was a kid helping an adult, and she felt proud for the same reason. "Oh, Mrs. Spencer, I'm so sorry. I don't know what to say." Say anything! "Have you heard from Kim or Mr. Spencer? Is she all right? Has Mr. Spencer gotten any help for Kim?"

Mrs. Spencer pulled a much crumpled handkerchief from her uniform pocket and wiped her eyes. She faced Erica and said, "Kim's in the hospital where he lives."

"A hospital!"

The terrible news gushed. "Jim came over as soon as he could. It was midnight when he got here. He ranted on and on. How could I have let this happen? What kind of a mother was I?" She looked at Erica as if waiting for a reply. "He told me there were better doctors and facilities where he lives. He is right, you know. Our hospital doesn't have the kind of programs they have near Jim's home. They have a very reputable eating disorders clinic there so, you know, he is right." Mrs. Spencer paused for a long while then added bitterly, "He's always been right on everything."

"Well not about you." Erica seized the opportunity. "You're one of the nicest people I know…" Once again, Erica stroked the woman's back. She hoped Mrs. Spencer believed her. How come Mr. Spencer always seemed like the good guy? He wasn't. Aloud Erica finished with a more polite thought: "And you're the best mother I know, outside of my own, and I mean that, Mrs. Spencer."

Mrs. Spencer heaved a sigh. "Well, thank you for saying so, Erica...I think I *will* believe you," she laughed wistfully, "because I sure could use something to make me feel better right now."

During the peaceful silence that followed Erica contemplated the woman next to her. Late thirty-something just like her own mother, Mrs. Spencer was attractive despite her large size. Her short dark hair, neatly styled, complimented her well-groomed appearance. Her warmth and concern, though sometimes excessive, made Mrs. Spencer a wonderful person. What power did Mr. Spencer possess that made her think so poorly of herself? She was a supervising nurse. How was it he could make her feel so unsure, so inadequate, until she actually behaved that way? Privately Erica declared Mr. Spencer a jerk for giving her up. Out loud, she asked, "Mrs. Spencer, is Kim any better?"

Mrs. Spencer cupped Erica's hands into her own and tried to smile. "I spoke with her yesterday. She sounded so young...like a little girl again. She said she's feeling better. They had her on intravenous, but Jim told me she may be getting clear liquids soon."

"What do you mean, Mrs. Spencer?" Erica cried. "Can't she eat?"

At first Kim's mother hesitated to speak, feeling as though she were confessing. "Kim hasn't been eating much. It's been such a long time, she hasn't been able to keep anything down." Collapsing her head into her hands again she cried. "It's all my fault. I knew Kim was lying to me." She lifted her head up and continued. "When she came back from Jim's this summer she would say it was too hot to eat. When school started and I was home to eat with her, she'd barely pick at her food telling me she ate big lunches at school. When I worked evenings she'd tell me she'd eaten…I had no way of knowing." She paused briefly. "But I did know!" she cried hysterically. "I just didn't know what to do…how to confront her. I was so afraid I'd lose her."

Erica gently stroked the sobbing woman's hair. Minutes passed and the two were once again sitting quietly, holding hands, offering each other vague reassurance. After a solemn good-bye, Erica rode her bike homeward with none of the energy with which she had begun her journey. She wondered what made people like Mrs. Spencer keep everything inside until something terrible forced them to speak. She hoped that by the time she became an adult she would know how to express her feelings—or at least find someone like a Marilyn Grayson if she didn't know how.

XVI
Marilyn Grayson

"I hate my schedule I hate hate hate my schedule!" Erica fumed as her mother drove half-listening to her daughter's ongoing complaints. The night before, Erica had phoned Jeanna's house constantly but no one answered. When someone finally picked up at ten thirty, it was Jeanna's father curtly stating it was far too late for phone calls. "Of all days to miss the bus I had to pick this one. Now I have to wait till eighth hour to talk to Jeanna. Ugh, I hate my schedule!"

During first period, Erica's mood brightened when Mrs. Bouton announced: "Okay, everybody, attention. We're having a special assembly this morning. We will be joined in the lecture hall by Mr. Hawk's class to hear a guest speaker today. Take your books with you because this assembly will last through second hour."

It must be Marilyn! Erica ignored the student clamor of *excellents* and *awesomes* as well as Mrs. Bouton's ensuing reprimands. Why didn't Mom tell me it was today? Oh, right. She feels guilty I even knew about it at all. Erica closed her notebook and pulled her bag from the rack below her chair. In just a few minutes she would be able to see Jeanna and tell her what she had learned about Kim. Suddenly Erica stopped. If Marilyn Grayson was the guest speaker, her most important audience member, Kim, would not be present. She finished gathering her belongings more slowly.

Mrs. Bouton led them past the gym where they were joined by Mr. Hawks' class. Jeanna found Erica first. "Boy, my dad was ticked at you for calling so late last night. What's up?"

As they walked to the lecture hall Erica told Jeanna about her visit with Mrs. Spencer. Erica measured each of Jeanna's responses, making sure she understood all that had occurred. By the time she finished, they were sitting in the front row of the auditorium. "Have you figured out yet who our speaker is?"

"Grayson," Jeanna answered. Erica remained silent which prompted Jeanna's understanding. She grabbed Erica's wrist and cried, "Oh, gawd, Erica. Kim's not here!"

✼✼✼✼✼✼✼

"Good morning, ladies," Marilyn said brightly as she stepped onto the stage, her heels striking the floor sharply. "And gentleman," she quickly added, acknowledging Mr. Hawks. "I understand, Mr. Hawks, you are the first male teacher of a female PE and Health class here. My congratulations."

Blushing, Mr. Hawks nodded. The buzzing crowd of students, happy to miss a class for any reason, slowly quieted for Marilyn who waited patiently and enthusiastically.

Erica smiled hopefully. Marilyn Grayson was everything her mother had said and more. She was tall, almost muscular. Her dramatic makeup flattered her cocoa brown skin. A wide leather belt with colorful beads and coppery metal swirls clasped tightly at the waist of her tan jumpsuit. She spoke with the confidence of a successful talk show host.

Erica's hand caught Mrs. Bouton's attention. "What kind of material is her outfit made out of? It looks like thin burlap," she whispered.

Mrs. Bouton arched her brow disapprovingly and said, "I think it's raw silk, Erica, and I am certain you're not here to study textiles."

Satisfied, Erica ignored the sarcastic reprimand.

Marilyn introduced herself to the students as a psychotherapist who had spoken at their high school for several years. It was a pleasure for her to speak to the freshmen audience she said, adding, "I believe it's very important that I speak to as many young adults as I can."

Marilyn shifted her weight from the stool onto which she had seated herself and with four steps left the stage to walk among the students. Oh how I wish Kim were here! Erica was certain this woman she so eagerly watched could have helped Kim. If only there was more time.

When the hush she waited for arrived, Marilyn Grayson addressed her audience. "I'd like you all to look around at each other and ask yourselves: Who's the prettiest person here?"

Erica grinned sheepishly but followed the instruction just as, she noticed, everyone else was.

"How many of you...be honest," she chuckled. "How many of you chose yourself as the prettiest?"

Now the audience laughed, whispered, or squealed mutterings that verified no one, of course, had.

Marilyn smiled as she once again waited for quiet. "I want to share with you today—a little bit about myself." Marilyn lingered on almost every word, stretching syllables like an actress and politician all at once. "And I want to talk to you a little bit about body image…about self-esteem."

Marilyn Grayson sauntered up and down the aisles. "What made you decide who was the prettiest person in this room?" she asked. "Think about it. Was it an image you conjured up all by yourself?" (Laughter. Quiet.) "Was it an image your parents may have suggested?" (More laughter. Eventually quiet.) "Was it an image you saw on television or in a magazine?" (Whispers. Whispers.) "Ahhh," Marilyn sang dramatically. "I think we've found one of the culprits." Erica was fascinated. Her concern for Kim momentarily vanished. Marilyn was speaking to her.

"I want to talk today about what can happen when you entrust your body and self-image to someone or something outside yourself. About what can happen when you have small or large problems…and you isolate your problems…and you try to isolate yourself…from outside help."

****

The ninety minutes flew by too rapidly. When Mr. Hawks directed the assembly of girls to their third hour classes, they moaned protests and ignored him. They surrounded Marilyn who by now sat on the stage listening to and answering their questions. When Marilyn got up they rose, some of them waiting in a line that spontaneously formed. So many wanted to speak with her or hug her or ask for her business card. Across the aisles Mr. Hawks and Mrs. Bouton shrugged and smiled at each other giving in to the girls' needs.

Erica waited, too. When she finally reached Marilyn she identified herself and thanked her. "Oh, Erica, I'm so happy to meet you!" Erica blushed. The last thing Erica expected or wanted was outright familiarity. "You look so much like your mother," Marilyn squealed with delight as she hugged Erica warmly.

In spite of her embarrassment Erica remained. She complimented Marilyn whose perfume, Erica noted, was heavy yet pleasing. "You were wonderful...I mean...really. Everything you shared about yourself...how heavy you were...how important it is for us to know how to take care of ourselves physically and mentally...I just wish..." Her voice trailed off but Marilyn's gentle nod encouraged her to finish. "I just wish my friend, Kim, could have been here to hear you."

Marilyn set aside her exuberant demeanor. She embraced Erica and whispered, "I understand, Erica...I know. Me, too."

When the line dwindled to a few girls Mrs. Bouton shouted, "All right, ladies, line up by the door. You will be able to contact Ms. Grayson at the number on her card. You have got to get to your third hour class now or you will earn yourselves tardies."

The group finally acquiesced, more because they realized the boys gym classes were now filing into the hall than because of Mrs. Bouton's order. As the last few girls shuffled through the open doors, one yelled, "WE LOVE YOU!"

Unabashed, Marilyn yelled back, "I love you, too, darlings!"

❋❋❋❋❋❋❋

The lunchroom noise focused on the morning's guest speaker. *"Can you believe she lost one hundred pounds? She's so gorgeous!"..."I'm going to ask my parents if I can go to her because she's great."..."She understands exactly how I feel."..."I need someone like that to talk to."..."I need help!"...*Erica listened with satisfaction. So many of her friends felt better today. Felt better about themselves. She did, too. She waved expectantly to Steve and Richie who were stalled on the snack line, when she heard a familiar voice. "Erica, can I sit with you?"

"Yes, Amy," Erica answered flatly.

"That lady said a lot of stuff today that Kim should have heard."

"Duh," Erica groaned.

"But how can we get Kim to hear it, Erica?" Amy persisted. "There's no way of reaching her. I've tried and Jenell tried, but all we get is the answering machine."

"Well, hello, ladies. You two talking?...Great. Move over and make way for two handsome studs," laughed Steve.

Amy welcomed the friendly interruption and giggled. "One workshop with a shrink and you think you're God's gift already?"

"May-be," he laughed. "That lady was great...I mean it. And funny, too." The chair scraped loudly against the floor as he maneuvered to straddle it. "At first I thought the whole thing was gonna be lame, really lame," he claimed resting his folded arms comfortably on the back of his chair. "But, man, she had us thinking in there, right, Rich?" Sorting the diced carrots away from the corn on his plate, Richie only nodded.

"Why so down, Richie?" Amy asked. Erica kicked Amy's leg under the table and Amy understood why when Richie said, "Oh, it's nothing. I just wish Kim could have been there, that's all." He paused then added too loudly, "She's the one who needed to hear about deadly diets." The group of students at the adjacent table turned and watched knowingly. He lowered his voice and continued. "She's the one who needed to hear about reachin' out for help with family problems...self-esteem...support groups...all that crap—"

"It wasn't crap, Richie," Amy interrupted.

"Shut up, Amy!" Erica and Steve said in unison.

Marilyn Grayson had opened their eyes to something they hadn't understood until now. Kim had concealed her physical and mental condition with too many veils of disguise. Now she lay alone suffocating under a self-made shroud of deception. Was it too late to help her?

Quietly they sat, picking at their food until at last Erica realized she could at least share what she knew about Kim's condition. She manufactured a reassuring tone. "Hey, you guys. I spoke with Mrs. Spencer yesterday."

Erica's friends leaned forward eagerly. Any news was better than none. It was a connection to their troubled friend, and it offered consolation. And maybe hope.

XVII
Grandpa

Erica knocked on the door with her foot as she searched impatiently for her keys. Philip opened the door just as she found them. "Hi, Erica," he said flatly tightening his grip on Diamond who struggled to free himself from the one-armed stranglehold Philip used to open the door.

"What's the matter, honey bunch? It's Friday."

"Grandpa's sick. Mommy's sad," Philip whimpered, tightly embracing the fidgeting cat.

"Mom's home already?" she asked. Without waiting for an answer Erica rushed to the kitchen. Gail, who had obviously been crying, sat at the kitchen counter holding a coffee mug against her chin. When she saw Erica her eyes filled with tears.

"Grandpa's sick, Erica," she said with forced calm. "They said not to come tonight, but I'm going first thing tomorrow. You don't have to come—"

"No!" Erica cried as she rushed to her mother and hugged her. "Of course I have to come...Philip, too. We love Grandpa...What's the matter with him?"

"I don't know. Shady Lodge called me at work. They said Grandpa complained about chest pains last night so they placed him in their infirmary for observation just in case it's his heart."

"Mom…don't worry. It can be nothing." Erica needed to sound cheerful for both their sakes. "It can be indigestion. You know Grandpa eats all the wrong foods…Mom, please don't worry."

"I know, I know…" Gail's attempted smile crumbled. "It's just that I can't do it again! I can't! My husband, my mother…That accident took so much from me…I can't go through it again!…He's all, he's all…" Setting the mug down heavily, she folded her arms and dropped her head into them.

Erica massaged her mother's shoulders. She leaned over and whispered, "You have Philip and me, mom. You'll always have us."

Gail lifted her head, wiped her eyes and assembled a smile. "You're right, Erica. I didn't mean…." She paused, caressing Erica's cheek gently. "You're absolutely right, angel." Yanking a fresh tissue from the almost empty box, Gail blew her nose hard. "And since we can't do anything until tomorrow anyway," she took a deep breath, "why don't you tell me how Marilyn's talk went."

Remembering how eager she had been to share the day's events, Erica happily obliged her mother.

XVIII
Shady Lodge

The forty minute drive to the Shady Lodge Adult Home was filled with license plate bingo, state capital trivia, and follow-ups on last night's impromptu debate. "But Mom, the hospital's only ten minutes away from Grandpa. I really want to see Kim if they'll let me in." Erica's pleas had been ongoing and thus far futile.

"I keep telling you, Erica, it is a lot longer than ten minutes and until I see how my father is, I don't care about Kim."

Gail scanned her rear view mirror and changed lanes, mumbling an impatient epithet at the car in front of her and a silent one at her daughter.

Though Erica felt bad about her grandfather, she wasn't as worried as her mother. Grandpa was strong and funny; of course he was fine. I bet he's sick because he ate too much. Erica automatically shook her head at the irony that her best friend was sick because she *didn't* eat enough.

The fiery autumn colors that bordered the expressway consoled her. Shifting her focus to a stare, the leaves became a kaleidoscopic swirl of colors. She turned around to tell Philip about this special view, but he was already staring out the window so spellbound, she wondered if he hadn't already discovered the phenomenon.

✸✸✸✸✸✸✸

An attractive woman wearing a red linen suit walked toward them as soon as they entered the lobby. Her high heels echoed on the shiny flagstone floor.

"Hello, Mrs. Shepherd," she said brightly as she enfolded Gail's outreached hand into hers. "I'm so happy I can tell you your father is feeling better this morning. I tried to reach you, but apparently you had already left your house. His doctor is very optimistic that his discomfort was nothing more than a bad case of indigestion."

"Oh, I'm so relieved!" Gail cried as she embraced the adult home's director.

"See, I told you, Mom," Erica cheered. She picked Philip up and swung him around.

"Yeah, Mom, I told you," Philip parroted adding, "What, Erica?"

Erica laughed and declared: "That Grandpa is going to be just fine."

"Yeah, Mom, I told you," Philip repeated.

Erica knew she would have to wait while Philip and her mother visited first. She didn't mind the infirmary rule that allowed only two visitors at one time. She remembered, not fondly, how small and musty the room was last time her grandfather was there for bronchitis; but she also remembered how much she enjoyed being alone with him when it was her time. Sharing him with no one, she listened to special stories about her grandmother and her parents that he never seemed to share when her mother was around.

Erica strolled through the lobby admiring the resident artwork displayed on easels that stood adjacent to lush green plants. She'd been half-listening to a pleasant piano tune and singing voices. She looked through the enormous glass wall that separated the lobby from the recreation center and saw a group of elderly people smiling wrinkled smiles, singing along with a silver-haired pianist: *"You're nobody till somebody loves you, so find yourself somebody to love."*

Something about the scene seemed strangely familiar to Erica. Suddenly she remembered—gasped: "I don't believe it"—and rushed into the room.

The song ended and the small group of singers laughed and patted each other approvingly. Some still tapped their feet. Erica walked directly to the pianist, smiling sheepishly at the old woman whose face seemed decorated with powdery circles, the softest shade of peach, on each cheek. "Hello. My name is Erica Shepherd," she said quickly before she lost her nerve. "You play very nicely...I play the piano, too...Well...I mean I don't play like you, but I take lessons." She felt thoroughly foolish. Idiot, stop talking so fast. Calm down!

The woman unknowingly rescued Erica from the awkward moment. "Well, thank you, Erica. My name is Mars Perri, and I'm flattered to be complimented by a fellow pianist."

I knew it I knew it I knew it I knew it! Erica privately squealed. It was Mars, the woman in Kim's diary! Not only did she feel close to the old woman seated before her, she felt close, closer to Kim, than she had for a long time.

"I don't know if you'd remember…" Erica started hesitantly. "A friend of mine…a girl about my height…but real thin…with blonde hair…met you here this summer. She listened to you play and talked with you. Her name was—"

"Kim. Kim Spencer. Yes, of course I remember her." Mars raised her hands to her cheeks and rocked. "I don't have that many young fans that I'd forget such a sweet thing." She winked impishly. "And I'm not so old I can't remember a compliment," Mars added quickly running her fingers up the keyboard's highest notes.

Erica could barely contain her gushing excitement, but her toothy grin faded when the pronounced blue veins of the woman's bony hands returning to the keyboard distracted her. In those quiet seconds Erica made a decision. "Mars, my friend's sick." She leaned on the piano. Shocked by the urge to confide in a complete stranger, her words poured nonetheless. About Kim's anger at her parents, fights with her friends, her diet, her anorexia, her hospitalization. Even as she spoke, Erica debated whether she should continue, but she could not stop. She spoke feverishly to Mars whose eyes seemed attentive, while her trembling hands rested on chords that, at any moment, surely would resound.

Erica realized that at some point she had also begun to reveal the secret wishes she normally concealed in her own diary. The wish that she could be happy with her body. Not always start diets doomed at their outset by her very own resistance to their need.

Wishes that her father were still alive so she could be part of a real family again. Wishes that she didn't worry so much about her mother, her brother, and everyone! all the time. She was so tired of it. Exposing her thoughts to a person was so different from writing them. So strange. She felt a wash of relief.

When Erica stopped talking she half expected her patient listener to point out how much she had complained. Point out that she should be proud of her figure which would be welcomed in any "large and lovely" catalog. That she was lucky she still had a mother and brother to worry about. That no one was asking her to worry about them or carry their burdens in the first place! She knew her own mind chastised and advised her now and not the silent old woman. But why now and never when she wrote about these feelings? Now, when she had said them out loud to someone? Though she could not answer her questions, she felt another comforting wash of relief.

Only when a long silence had rooted itself did Mars close her eyes and finally begin her music. She gently swayed, dancing with the melody, perhaps reliving some half forgotten moment. Her palsied eyebrow twitched a beat at odds with the tune's.

Erica frowned. Was the woman senile? She had said nothing all the while Erica had spoken. At first she believed Mars had remained politely quiet and would eventually respond. But now Erica suspected Mars had merely waited for the babble to end so that she could resume playing. "That's a pretty song," Erica said. She privately consoled herself. She had at least vented and felt better for it. Besides, no one she knew had been present to see her make a complete and total fool of herself. "I think I heard that song in a movie."

"Rachmaninoff," Mars whispered. She opened her eyes and continued. "And I wouldn't be a bit surprised if you recognized it from a wonderfully romantic movie, *Somewhere in Time.*"

"Yeah...Maybe that's it," Erica said politely, although she wasn't really sure that was the movie—or that she cared.

Mars nodded, intertwining the melody with a melodramatic account of the movie. "It's a story of an elderly woman...who longs to recapture her youth and her lover...but in trying, loses them both."

"Yes, I think I did see that," Erica said, momentarily forgetting that Mars had ignored her own painful soliloquy. "Gosh, you play beautifully. I can never talk and play at the same time...not unless it's chopsticks or something."

"To play this well..." Mars had reached the piece's highest point and stopped speaking. When she was finished, as though it were but a second ago, she completed her sentence: "you must practice until it hurts."

"That's just what you said to Kim!" Erica said recalling Kim's diary, but she was not sure Mars heard her over the applause that had started respectful seconds after the piece had ended.

Mars graciously nodded to her audience then cast an authoritative stare on Erica and declared: "That's what I tell *all* my pupils. I taught music, you know."

"Yes, I know. That's very nice." Erica glanced into the lobby and then at her watch. "Uh, I have to go now.

It's almost time for me to visit my grandfather. You might know him...Peter Flanagan?"

"Well, dearie, I'm not sure I do. I might, but I'm not much good with names around here."

Erica nodded a sullen smile and almost turned to walk away when Mars offered a sudden and unexpected flurry of welcomed commentary. "You tell Kim for me she's a lovely girl because she's lovely *inside*." Mars pointed to her heart. Erica eagerly responded when Mars shifted in her seat, her patting fingers inviting Erica to sit beside her. "Tell her I've missed her phone calls. Tell her Mars wants her to stop her diet and eat something...so she can visit me again...enjoy my music...and tell me how wonderfully I play...As for you, young lady..." Mars looked at Erica warmly and whispered, "Relax a little. You can't worry about everybody...Live your own life. Enjoy your own life. The world won't stop without you." She ended with a familiar, mischievous wink.

"That's what we need around here," Mars said with a strength in her voice that crescendoed: "Young people telling us how wonderful we are. Isn't that right, everybody?" Mars faced her gray-haired audience for their approval.

Erica's hand covered her mouth to stifle a threatening sob. Tears glistened in her eyes as the elderly people seated before the piano smiled wide grins—some toothless—nodding and voicing their unanimous agreement. Mars gently took Erica's hand away from her mouth and patted it gently as she spoke. "You come talk to me whenever you like, young lady, and Kim, too, when she feels better...Okay everyone: Show time!" Her advice ending as abruptly and unexpectedly as it had begun, Mars challenged her peers: "See if you can keep up with this one."

The plinkety-plink notes that heralded *New York, New York* rose from the piano and filtered through the musty air like magic. *"Start spreading the news..."*

Erica quickly kissed the fragrant peach circle on Mars' cheek and practically danced her way to the lobby. Mars had remembered Kim. And she cared enough about Kim—and her—to offer what sounded like good advice. By the time she got to see her grandfather she was overjoyed.

"How's my petunia?" he asked, holding his arms out to his granddaughter.

She rushed to his bedside and gushed, "I'm fine, Grandpa Flanagan. I couldn't be better!"

XIX
Message from Mars

Erica's cheek muscles ached from the smile that refused to leave her face. Could this day get any better? In less than a minute she had persuaded her mother to take her to see Kim; and though Kim might not be happy to see her at first, Erica was confident she soon would be. After all: she had a message from Mars.

When they drove up the circular driveway that led to the hospital's parking area, Gail let out a whistle. "Holy…This place looks more like a hotel than a hospital!"

"Mrs. Spencer told me it's one of the best around," Erica offered.

"I can believe it," Gail muttered as she turned into a parking space she'd spotted.

Erica secured a visitor's pass and waved it excitedly at her mother. Gail smiled and pointed to the cafeteria directly opposite the lobby desk. "I'll be in there with Philip. Now that I know grandpa's okay, I'm suddenly starving. Try not to be too long, honey. When you come down, you can get something to eat, too."

Erica okayed her mother repeatedly, anxious to head toward the elevator she'd been eyeing ever since she'd spotted it.

THIN VEILS

Butterflies teased her stomach as the elevator surged upward. She drew in a breath as the doors opened. Nervously she stepped forward. The fourth floor was colored with purple tweed carpeting, the walls, a lighter shade. A nurse at the desk nodded silently to the right when she held up her pass. She walked past three rooms and stopped by the door marked 403. She knocked lightly and entered.

Walking on the balls of her feet to Kim's bedside Erica stifled a gasp; Kim looked so frail. Oh, I can't wake her. But I have to. I want to talk to her, listen to her, tell her what Mars said! Hesitating a moment longer, Erica gently tapped Kim's shoulder and whispered, "Kim…Kim…"

Kim stirred. "Erica?" she murmured. "Is that you?"

Erica cheered, "Well, hey, that's great, you recognize me." Erica was ashamed of the discomfort she felt at the sight of Kim.

Kim opened her tired eyes and smiled slightly. "Of course I do."

"How are you, Kim?" Erica forced out perfunctorily. "Everybody misses you…Oh, Kim," she sighed, finally at ease, "I'm so happy to see you! Amy and Jenell said to say they're so sorry…and Jeanna misses you like crazy…and Richie hates himself for the break up and for not knowing how to help you…and Steve, well…Steve is Steve. You know how he feels."

Kim was tired, so tired. But her friend's trademark chatter brought a smile to her lips as she listened with closed eyes. When Erica stopped, Kim ordered her eyes to open; slowly they cooperated. She was tired, so tired. Her voice, a whisper. "I really messed up, didn't I?"

"No, of course not. What do you mean? You're going to be fine," Erica quietly insisted though she was terribly afraid. "It'll just take some time."

"Yeah...time." Kim slowly rolled her head away from Erica and stared out the tall window beside her bed. "My dad says I'll be staying with him if...when...I get out of here. She was barely audible. "I'll be an outpatient so I can still see my counselor." She began to turn her head back to catch a glimpse of Erica but she was so tired. "He's a nice guy. Cute, too," she added, barely audible.

Erica smiled but privately ached. Kim looked so fragile. She regretted Kim had gotten sick before Marilyn Grayson spoke at their school. Maybe, just maybe, the workshop would have been enough to help Kim, although by now Erica knew better. Maybe this was the way it had to be. Would this hospital help her? Kim looked so bad. "Hey...guess who else sends a hello?" Erica asked hopefully. She interpreted the slight movement of Kim's head for *who?* Though mentioning Mars was a gamble—surely it would remind Kim that Erica had invaded the privacy of her diary—it was a worthwhile gamble. "Mars."

This time Kim did work to turn her head back towards Erica. When she saw Kim's smile, Erica realized she had been holding her breath because she exhaled so deeply. Kim moved her body ever so slightly and Erica, sensing that Kim wanted to sit upright, assisted her by maneuvering pillows and IV lines, pressing the buttons of the motorized mattress until Kim lay in a reclining position.

"Where'd you see her? How do you even know her?" Kim murmured. Her smile faded. "Oh…yeah." Her delicate body sunk back into the pillows ever so slightly.

Erica held her breath again as she looked pleadingly at Kim. "So, tell me," Kim whispered, breaking the tension: "What did she say?"

Joy and relief radiated from Erica's face and she laughed. She held Kim's free hand in both of hers and spoke solemnly. "She said to tell you you're a lovely girl…because you're lovely inside…She says she wants you to stop your diet. She wants you to eat something and get well…so you can visit her again…" Erica's tone lightened, "and tell her how great she plays the piano!" Erica scooted up onto the bed.

"Did she really say that, Erica? She really remembered me?"

"Yes, Kim, really. Of course she would have. You're too special to forget. She also told me some things that I needed to hear."

"Like what?" Kim asked softly.

Erica struggled to find the right words. "She sort of told me it's okay to mind my own business."

Kim tilted her head, puzzled by Erica's words.

"Kim, I have to tell you something else…I've been thinking a lot about you and me lately, and there's something I need to say." Erica swallowed. "I've always admired you…envied you really…"

Oh, Erica—"

"No…really." Now it was Erica who turned away and looked out the window, speaking to golden green leaves and blue sky. "You always seemed so perfect to me. In all the years I've known you, I've never even seen you with a zit." She swallowed a lump in her throat and turned, sharing a smiling moment with Kim before her face grew somber. "I have to confess, Kim...I was angry at you for wanting to lose weight...Oh, I was worried, too, Kim...You know that! You have to know that. But I was angry,...because I was jealous...I just wanted to tell you." Erica's tear-filled eyes retreated to the safer view the window offered.

"I wish I could have been there for you when you needed help, Kim...and I'd try again if I had to...Maybe we all need to find our own help. Even if it means finding it the hard way. Kim, I do hope they're helping you here. Anyway, I just wanted to tell you the whole truth."

Erica continued to speak more to herself than to Kim who had again closed her eyes. She remembered her time with Mars. "I'm always trying to help everyone when it's me I need to help. I'm always going around telling everybody they should accept themselves for who they are, the *way* they are." Erica slumped back and smiled. "I think maybe I'd better start believing that myself." When Erica turned, she saw tears glistening on Kim's lashes. "Kim, what's wrong?" Erica hopped off the bed and hovered close to her friend. "What's wrong?"

"Nothing. Everything." Kim gently tightened her grasp on her friend's hand, while Erica used the back of her free hand to wipe a tear from Kim's cheek. Kim's eyes remained closed and she spoke with much difficulty. "You were jealous of me," she said weakly. "That's funny, Erica. For so long I went out of my way to be mean to you, because...I was...jealous of you...now you're saying you were jealous of me...That's messed up, Erica." Kim's fragile body succumbed to a racking cough just as a nurse entered.

"Kim, are you all right?" The nurse glared accusingly at Erica.

"We were just talking and—"

"Well, I'm afraid you need to leave, young lady," she snapped then immediately shifted to a pleasant tone. "Kim, dear," she said as she rubbed Kim's back and coaxed her through sips of what looked like lime water. "I think you may have had a little too much excitement."

"One more minute," Kim managed. "Please."

Concerned about Kim's less than favorable response to treatment, the nurse decided to oblige her young patient. "Of course, Kim," she smiled. "But, young lady—" She turned to Erica and arched an intimidating eyebrow: "One more minute means one more minute."

"Yes, m'am," Erica said politely as the nurse retreated. Erica reestablished her position on Kim's bed.

Kim heaved a sigh. "All those times I was mean to you—"

"Oh, Kim, don't. I know—"

"No you don't, Erica. Be quiet...I didn't know myself...not then anyway. Now that I'm here," she continued in the same soft but important tone, "I'm learning about myself.

"I was mean to you...for a long time, Erica...because I was jealous. I was the one who was jealous. Jealous of what you have...your mom, your brother. Your family."

"But, Kim, I don't have a father."

"Yeah. But you're still a family. You don't need two parents to feel like you have…family…No matter." Kim closed her eyes, her delicate body dwarfed by the layer of pillows that cushioned it. Erica eased herself from the bed. She solemnly studied Kim's peaceful face as her fingers groped for the panel fastened to the bed's metal bars. A motor droned, lowering the bed to its reclining position. A comfortable quiet, known only to close friends, followed. Finally Kim spoke. "I'd like to talk with Mars again."

"Maybe your dad will take you to Shady Lodge when you're stronger."

"I could call her again."

"Of course you could," Erica immediately replied, reminded of the phone calls Mars had mentioned. She wondered how often Kim had talked with Mars, what they talked about, if Kim had spoken about her diet. Knowing it was better not to ask, Erica said, "I'm sure she'd love to hear from you, Kim…" then, adding for herself, "Maybe I'll call her, too."

✸✸✸✸✸✸✸

Erica had hoped to end her visit with a few minutes of what Philip would have called "girl talk." Instead she kissed Kim's forehead, whispered I love you and left the room promising to return. She nodded a thank you to the nurse.

She waited for the elevator, anguished by the visit, so different from what she had hoped for. She thought about the Spencers, their constant battles, their divorce, their game of tug o' war that had stretched Kim's emotions, and now her health, dangerously thin. A sweet old lady, a stranger really, thought Erica, was the only person who had offered Kim a measure of what she needed. Like a referee blowing a whistle, Mars had provided Kim a much needed time out. But when Kim's deadly game began, the ref had left the playing field. Erica stepped into the elevator wondering what whistle Mars had blown for her. The doors closed.

When the doors opened, Erica was privately clinging to the wistful smile that had crept across Kim's face when she heard Erica promise to visit again—next time—with the whole crew.

XX
The Gym

Monday afternoon Jeanna and Erica hurried to the gym. They had to find the least expensive way to decorate for Friday night's Harvest Dance. Several committee members, already there, discussed the floor plan for the DJ, concession stand, and dance area. "Hey, Erica! Jeanna!" Steve yelled as he waved a sweeping arm at them from across the gym. They waved back.

"Erica, I think we should just get some yellow and white construction paper from the art room, cut it into paper circles and stick the circles on the walls. Pretend they're moons. That'll be enough. Maybe some orange and green leaves, too. And maybe we should buy some corn shocks. This place is way too big to get complicated. Don't forget," Jeanna warned: "What goes up must come down...and I don't intend to do tons of work." Erica offered a series of maybes.

Arm in arm the two girls started twisting their sneakers into the gym floor, exaggerating the already syncopated squeaks. "Erica, do you think Kim will be back in time for the dance?"

"No way. From what her mother told me and my mom, Kim's going to be in the hospital for a long while, until some kind of count goes up...electrolytes or something."

Mrs. Spencer had also told them of Kim's poor response to treatment. But Erica, hopeful it was only a matter of time before Kim responded, chose not to share the depressing detail with her friend. "Even when she gets out," Erica continued, almost lightly, "Mrs. Spencer says Kim'll be on home tutoring at her dad's house so she can be an outpatient at the clinic there. Mr. Spencer thinks that since Sandy doesn't work, she can take care of Kim."

"Sandy?...Oh that really makes sense," Jeanna groaned.

"Jeanna..." Erica halted and faced her friend. "Kim has to get better first no matter what they decide."

"When will that be? When will they let her have more visitors? It's not fair you got to see her," Jeanna complained innocently.

"It's going to take time, Jeanna," Erica said reassuringly. "I keep telling you they thought I was related to her. That's the only reason they let me in...It won't be long," Erica added.

Erica heaved a sigh. She regretted her decision to protect her friends. Having returned from her visit with Kim and then Kim's mother without revealing the severity of Kim's condition to them, what else could she do, but continue the lie? Why should my friends have to worry as much as me she had thought. At the time it seemed like the right thing to do. "Let's just pray it will be soon," Erica heard herself say, "and that the hospital okays visits again so we all can see her. I know that will make Kim feel better." Genuinely believing what she had just said, Erica nudged Jeanna back into stride.

From the moment Steve's hello had caught her attention, Erica had been distracted by his body; it seemed to be shining. As she listened to Jeanna and spoken herself, Erica had stared at him believing she was mistaken. But as they crossed the double sized gym, the shine steadily increased. She had almost reached him when she understood. "What the hell do you have on, Steve?" she demanded.

"A plastic sweat suit. I'm jogging after this meeting," Steve answered smugly.

Erica assaulted Steve with curt phrases, each threaded to the next with its own accusing, questioning tone: "Why...are you wearing...a plastic sweat suit...in the gym...during a dance committee meeting?"

"I'm almost down to weight."

"WHAT?!"

"I said," Steve paused, trying to match Erica's indicting tempo with his one of his own, "I'm almost...down...to weight." He lost it when he added proudly, "I'm gonna make the wrestling team...I'm sure of it!"

"After all we've been through with Kim, you were dieting all this time?"

"Like I was really going to tell you, Erica!" Steve countered.

Erica was stunned. "After what happened to Kim? Our best friend?

"Well, I think it's cool, Steve. I hope you make it."

Erica's jaw dropped and her fists automatically tightened when she heard Jeanna. Had they both forgotten Kim and what happened to her? Had they forgotten everything Marilyn Grayson had said? Had they learned nothing?

"Hey, you guys," Richie called from across the gym. "No more loafing around. I'm here now. Get to work before I fire you all!" His playful shout broke the tension that locked the three together.

Erica turned and blew a long breath. What can I do? As if in reply, a shrill whistle blew. For Richie, the whistle signaled the entrance of the boys basketball team directly behind him, and he good-naturedly looked over his shoulder and quickened his step in mock fear. For Erica, the whistle signaled a reminder of Mars, calling a time out—for her: *The world won't stop without you.* Erica caught sight of one of the thunking basketballs, its blue and white school colors whirling around. It became for her a blue-white sphere, a world destined to rotate—without her help. She bit the corner of her lip wondering what she should say. She forced a smile.

Epilogue

Erica sat in the waiting room privately arguing with herself. Why did you come here, she kept asking. Because you made an appointment to come, that's why. She was distracted by the girl who had just passed through the waiting room from Marilyn's office. Why is she here? She looks normal. She doesn't look anorexic, overweight, messed up. I'm way heavy compared to her.

Leaning her elbows heavily into her thighs, her chin resting on open fists, Erica brooded. She was so angry at herself for gaining ten pounds. Ten pounds in ten days since Kim's death! She was embarrassed by it too. Why was she eating so much? How could she! Normal people didn't feel like eating when someone close died. I didn't eat more when Daddy died, she silently protested.

She looked up. Marilyn opened her office door, smiling a patient-client smile Erica thought cynically then guiltily. "I don't know why I'm here," she blurted as she stood. "I'm sorry, but I think I might be wasting your time."

"Not at all, Erica," Marilyn replied. "Lots of visits start out this way. You're fine."

The decor of Marilyn's office was as pleasing to Erica as the waiting room. "This is nice," she said. "I mean this room, your place, I mean—"

"Thank you, Erica," Marilyn said brightly, ignoring Erica's awkwardness. "Please, Erica, sit down."

THIN VEILS

Erica sat obligingly and Marilyn sat opposite her. She leaned forward, her eyes and posture silently encouraging Erica to speak.

"You know I gained ten pounds, huh?"

"Yes, Erica. You told me when you called."

"I'm really mad about that...I can't believe it," Erica added, more for herself.

"Do you think your anger played a part in your gaining weight?"

"No! Food played a part in my gaining weight," she complained. "I'm sorry," Erica said apologetically, "I didn't mean to snap."

"Don't be sorry, Erica," Marilyn answered casually. "You're a reality based young lady. There's no question, food plays a part—"

"A part?!"

"Maybe even a big part," Marilyn respectfully added, working to calm Erica. "Tell me more about your anger."

"I told you—"

"Yes, I know about your weight gain, and I would be pretty bothered by a ten pound weight gain, too, but take your time...think about what you are feeling, Erica: Are you feeling angry about the gain, or are you feeling *bothered* by the gain?" Marilyn asked, expertly blending compassion with inquiry.

"I'm angry, Ms. Grayson." Erica didn't have to think about it. To her core she knew the answer. "I'm so angry I can't even talk to my friends or my mom or Philip without losing my temper, snapping their heads off, acting like a jerk." Tears welled in Erica's eyes and Marilyn shifted forward and gently touched her palm over Erica's wringing hands until they settled.

"Will you talk about your anger, Erica?" Marilyn asked.

"I'm angry at Kim! There I said it." Erica was stunned. How freely the truth she had kept locked up for days, that had kept her locked up for days, had left her lips. She cried hard with relief. Marilyn settled back in her chair allowing this important time. She repositioned the box of tissues on the glass table beside Erica's chair, and Erica smiled as she reached for several, grateful for the cue that tissues were available.

When she sensed she could speak without crying, Erica heaved a sigh of relief. "Wow," she said half giggling, her smiling face aglow. "That was something, huh?"

Marilyn responded with a smile that offered acceptance, concern, understanding. Everything Erica needed.

Finally someone spoke. "Do you know why you're angry at Kim?" Marilyn asked "I don't mean anger because she died." Erica's smile disappeared. "I mean the anger you won't accept...that perhaps you're forcing down. Forcing down with food, maybe."

Erica drew a deep breath. "Wow," she exhaled. That was it. Erica thought she had been winning against the guilty thoughts that plagued her, but she realized now she had been losing.

Marilyn sensed the opportunity. "Erica, pretend you're writing a journal entry and you title it: 'I'm angry.'"

Erica listened hard though Marilyn's tone was almost light, as if she were beginning a children's story that Erica might finish. "The very first words you write are: 'I'm angry at Kim because she died.' Now, what comes next?" Marilyn stopped and leaned forward, eagerly awaiting the rest of the story.

****

A Guide to Understanding

Dear Reader,

Though Kim Spencer is a fictional character, Kim's problem is not. Eating disorders are epidemic in our country. It is reported that as many as ten million adolescents suffer nationwide and that dieting begins as early as third grade!

I wrote this guide to encourage and promote reflection and discussion concerning the issues that surround and consume the characters within my novel. I hope the guide helps you, as someone who silently suffers from an eating disorder, or as a friend who looks on helplessly.

Note: Questions are divided into three categories. Whole Group Discussion questions serve to recall and interpret events of each chapter. The Small Group Discussion and Journal Entry questions facilitate Small Group Discussion and reflective journal writing.

****

PRE-READING

≈ WHOLE GROUP DISCUSSION ≈
1. Based on the title, what is the book is about?
2. What does the cover suggest about the book and its characters?

PREFACE

≈ WHOLE GROUP DISCUSSION ≈
1. Has anyone ever dieted?
2. Have you ever known anyone who's dieted? Discuss the experience.
3. How does the preface prepare us for the book?

⋊⋉ SMALL GROUP DISCUSSION
How do innocent diets become deadly?

☯ JOURNAL ENTRY
What is more important to you: your health or your appearance? Why?

CHAPTER I

≈ WHOLE GROUP DISCUSSION ≈
1. How would you describe the relationship between Erica and Kim?
2. What are the first clues that alert Erica something is wrong?
3. What past events does Erica recall as she rides home on the school bus?

⋊⋉ SMALL GROUP DISCUSSION
Have you ever had a fight with a close friend? How did it start? End?

☯ JOURNAL ENTRY
Why do people close to us sometimes hurt our feelings?

CHAPTER II

≋ WHOLE GROUP DISCUSSION ≋

1. Describe Erica's relationship with Philip.
2. Why do you think Kim might be hostile toward Philip and Erica's relationship?
3. What does Erica learn after her phone conversation with Jeanna?
4. Describe Erica's relationship with her mother, Gail.
5. What do we learn about Erica based on her reflections on "Cynthia's Tea Party" and a baseball game from the past?

♓ SMALL GROUP DISCUSSION

1. How would you describe your relationships with your parents or guardians?
2. How difficult or easy is it to share your problems with your parents, guardians, or friends?

☯ JOURNAL ENTRY

Do you know the pain of losing a parent or know someone who has experienced such a loss? Reflect on the experience.

CHAPTERS III – IV

≋ WHOLE GROUP DISCUSSION ≋

1. Who is Steve and how is he significant to the characters and plot thus far?
2. How would you describe Erica's feelings about what has happened so far?
3. How does Kim react to Erica's "help" in the cafeteria?

4. What does Kim say to Erica that frightens her?

⚤ Small Group Discussion
1. Have you ever – or have you ever known someone who – dieted for a specific occasion or sport? What was the experience like emotionally and physically?
2. Kim lashes out at Erica, who believes she is only trying to help. When does caring become intrusion?

☯ Journal Entry
1. Have you ever been certain you were right while those around you believe otherwise?
2. Have you ever felt helpless?

CHAPTERS V – VI

≈ Whole Group Discussion ≈
1. Who is Marilyn Grayson and what role might she play?
2. What is the content of Erica's letter to Kim?
3. Why does the letter backfire?
4. What might Erica's search for her "oversized" sweater reveal about her?

⚤ Small Group Discussion
1. Why do close friends sometimes fight?
2. How does self-image and dieting affect mood and behavior?

THIN VEILS

☯ Journal Entry
Have you ever experienced an aching lump in your throat? What caused that pain?

CHAPTERS VII – VIII

≈ Whole Group Discussion ≈
1. What plan does Erica share with Jeanna?
2. Why does Jeanna resist at first?
3. How does Mrs.Spencer measure up to both Erica's and Jeanna's description?
4. How does Jeanna disarm Kim's initial coolness?
5. Why is Jeanna pleased, almost excited, about stealing Kim's diary?

♓ Small Group Discussion
How does Erica's relationship with her mother compare to Kim's relationship with her mother?

☯ Journal Entry
Is stealing or deception ever justifiable?

CHAPTER IX

≈ Whole Group Discussion ≈
1. How does Erica react to the theft of the diary?
2. Why does Erica finally agree to read the diary?
3. What do Kim's diary entries reveal about her? Her parents? The possible cause/s of her eating disorder?
4. Why is Kim attracted to the elderly woman named Mars whom she writes about?

⚣ SMALL GROUP DISCUSSION
Why is it sometimes easier to talk with strangers rather than people we are close to?

☯ JOURNAL ENTRY
1. Is reading another person's diary ever justifiable?
2. Has anyone ever invaded your privacy?
3. Have you ever invaded another's privacy? Why?

CHAPTERS X-XI

≋ WHOLE GROUP DISCUSSION ≋
1. What new insights do we learn about Kim's diet and her relationship with her mother Linda?
2. Although Kim expresses loving thoughts of her mother, she withholds them. Why?

⚣ SMALL GROUP DISCUSSION
1. Why do some daughters and sons find it difficult to express loving feelings to their parents and guardians?
2. Why do you think Linda Spencer remained silent rather than confront Kim with her suspicions about her eating patterns?

☯ JOURNAL ENTRY
Have you ever wanted to "speak out" and state how you really felt but could not?

CHAPTER XII

≋ WHOLE GROUP DISCUSSION ≋
1. How do Kim's friends react to Erica's concern for Kim?

THIN VEILS

2. What is Steve doing and why?
3. What does Steve say that hurts Erica?
4. Why is Steve unaware that he has hurt his friend, Erica?

♓ SMALL GROUP DISCUSSION

How do you feel about adults—coaches, for example—who impose strict eating and dieting expectations on their athletes?

☯ JOURNAL ENTRY

Do you ever wear masks or veils that hide the real you from your family and friends?

CHAPTERS XIII

≈ WHOLE GROUP DISCUSSION ≈

1. How does Erica deal with Kim in the weeks that follow the diary incident?
2. What signals do Kim's friends ignore that might have revealed her anorexia?
3. According to Mrs. Spencer's phone call, what happened to Kim at school?
4. Why does Gail get angry at Mrs. Spencer's reliance on her ex-husband?
5. Why is Jeanna worried about going over to Erica's house?
6. What can you theorize about Jeanna's parents?
7. How does news of Marilyn Grayson once again brighten Erica's spirits? How might Grayson help?

⚥ Small Group Discussion

1. Do you think that Erica and Richie should have done more than ignore Kim for two weeks? Was their behavior excusable given all they knew about Kim's secret diet club?
2. How soon should adults be advised about someone involved in extreme dieting?

☯ Journal Entry

1. How far do you believe allegiance to a friend should go?
2. Do you believe in tough love, which forces people to face their issues, addictions, disorders, etc. with or without their consent?

CHAPTER XIV

♒ Whole Group Discussion ♒

1. What does Erica learn from Amy and Jenell?
2. How would you answer Amy's question: "What could we have done?"

⚥ Small Group Discussion

1. What responsibilities and obligations do friends have to each other during personal crises?
2. To what extent if any are Amy and Jenell responsible for Kim's death?

☯ Journal Entry

Have you ever been betrayed? Have you ever betrayed?

CHAPTER XV

≋ WHOLE GROUP DISCUSSION ≋
1. Why have the Spencer household messages been left unanswered?
2. Why does Mrs. Spencer blame herself?
3. Why is Kim in a hospital near her father?
4. In what ways does Erica seem to be more adult than adolescent when she visits Mrs. Spencer?

⚹ SMALL GROUP DISCUSSION
1. What do we learn about Kim's father?
2. Is Kim's diary view of her father validated? Why or why not?

☯ JOURNAL ENTRY
Have you ever felt more adult than the adults around you?!

CHAPTER XVI

≋ WHOLE GROUP DISCUSSION ≋
1. Who is the guest speaker and what is the topic at the freshman class assembly?
2. Why is Richie angry at his friend's enthusiastic response to the assembly?

⚹ SMALL GROUP DISCUSSION
1. How does media negatively influence our daily lives?
2. How are you affected by the media image of "perfect"?

◉ JOURNAL ENTRY
How would your life be different if the media image of perfect did not exist?

CHAPTERS XVII – XVIII

〜 WHOLE GROUP DISCUSSION 〜
1. Why is Gail Shepherd upset when Erica returns home from school?
2. Why is Erica certain her grandfather is not seriously ill?
3. Why does Mars become so important to Erica?

♓ SMALL GROUP DISCUSSION
What is it about Mars Perri that helps to explain why Kim befriended and confided in her?

◉ JOURNAL ENTRY
1. Have you ever had a special confidante? Have you ever wished you had one?
2. Some of Erica's conviction that her grandfather is not seriously ill may come from her unwillingness to think otherwise. Have you ever been in denial about something?

CHAPTER XIX

〜 WHOLE GROUP DISCUSSION 〜
1. What does Erica confess to Kim at the hospital?
2. What does Kim confess to Erica?
3. Why won't Mars' simple idea "to eat" help Kim?

⧫ Small Group Discussion

1. What additional insights are revealed about Erica's issues and Kim's issues?
2. Are Erica's issues less important than Kim's?
3. What "whistle" do you think Mars may have blown for Erica? (Recall that Erica says Mars blew a time out for Kim)

☯ Journal Entry

1. Have you or someone you known ever suffered from an eating disorder or an eating disorder behavior?
2. Research anorexia and other eating disorders. What are the debilitating outcomes?

CHAPTER XX

≈ Whole Group Discussion ≈

1. Why are Erica and her friends in the gym?
2. What is Steve wearing that enrages Erica?
3. Why does Erica become furious with Steve and then Jeanna?
4. How does Erica ultimately handle her anger?

⧫ Small Group Discussion

How do you interpret Erica's smile at the end of the chapter?

☯ Journal Entry

How do you decide when to speak your mind and when to remain silent?

EPILOGUE

≈ WHOLE GROUP DISCUSSION ≈
1. Why is Erica in Marilyn Grayson's office?
2. How does Grayson respond to Erica's anger and denial?

♓ SMALL GROUP DISCUSSION
1. Why is it important to express our feelings?
2. What happens to friendship when dieting becomes deadly? Can the outcomes be prevented?

☯ JOURNAL ENTRY
What do you think Erica shares with Marilyn as she tells her story?

If you or anyone you know suffers from an eating disorder, please contact NEDA, the National Eating Disorders Association at :

1-800-931-2237 or at

www.NationalEatingDisorders.org

About the Author

A teacher of adolescents for seventeen years, Anne Hanson believes it is critical to explore the facts behind the fiction of *Thin Veils* to understand the physical and emotional damage caused by the eating disorders that victimize our nation's youth.

In addition National Board Certification in Early Adolescence/English Language Arts, Anne has garnered recognition as a member of Who's Who in America, Teacher of the Year 2000 finalist in Arizona, and Middle School Teacher of the Year 2002 in Scottsdale, where she currently resides and teaches.

Anne is also an educational consultant who has published two nonfiction books, one for teachers—*Write Brain Write* (The Brain Store, 2002), the other for students—*Visual Writing* (Learning Express, 2001).

Printed in the United States
129445LV00001B/97/A